THE MYSTERY OF THE MURDER THAT WASN'T

A Lady Darriby-Jones Mystery

CM RAWLINS

CleanTales Publishing

Copyright © CleanTales Publishing

First published in January 2024

All characters and events in this publication, other than those clearly in the public domain, are fictitious and any resemblance to real persons, living or dead, is purely coincidental.

Copyright © CleanTales Publishing

The moral right of the author has been asserted.

All rights reserved. This book or any portion thereof may not be reproduced or used in any manner whatsoever without the express written permission of the publisher except for the use of brief quotations in a book review.

For questions and comments about this book, please contact info@cleantales.com

ISBN: 9798876365750
Imprint: Independently Published

Other books in the A Lady Darriby-Jones Mystery series

The Mystery of the Polite Man

The Mystery of the American Slug

The Mystery of the Back Passage

The Mystery of the Murder that Wasn't

The Mystery of Miss Cess Pitt

The Mystery of the Missing Ladies

A Lady Darriby-Jones Mystery

BOOK FOUR

Chapter One

Whatever the weather, Lady Darriby-Jones considered as she waited by the car, it was impossible to be gloomy when Freddie was around.

Except, he wasn't around that particular Monday in mid-January and there was every chance they would miss his train, even with Smith putting the pedal to the floor, or whatever the expression was.

"Sorry auntie, I was just saying goodbye to Mrs Stone."

"Did she give you a little something for the journey?"

"Rather!" Freddie opened a large cloth napkin to reveal half-a-dozen sandwiches and the same number of fat round cupcakes with her famous red, white and blue icing designed like Union Jacks on each one.

"Put them in your overnight bag so you don't drop them, Freddie."

"There's already a chocy cake in there," he replied. "The biggest one you've ever seen. It's in a tin that takes up most of the available space." He pulled the zip, as if he had to evidence every statement to his 'aunt', actually his second cousin, once removed, and that only through marriage, for he was, correctly speaking, a blood relative of Lord Darriby, her husband, rather than of her.

"Milady?" said Smith, while indicating the time by placing two fingers on his wrist, causing considerable confusion with Lady Darriby-Jones.

"Are you feeling for your own pulse, Smith?" she asked.

"No," replied Freddie on Smith's behalf. "He's indicating that we need to get a move on or we'll miss the train. Come on, aunty, hop to it."

"The cheek of it," she muttered, but Freddie was already inside the car, having thrown his overnight bag in as if passing a rugger ball, actually achieving some spin so it hit the seat he was to occupy with incredible accuracy.

What damage it did to the chocolate cake, she would never know; presumably, it tasted the same whatever state it was in.

After a commentary delivered at top speed about running down the line, weaving past opponents for young Blythe to score yet again, right behind the posts, meaning when he took the conversion the kick was guaranteed, Lady Darriby-Jones was able to put in a question about the two fingers on the wrist trick.

"No, auntie, not a pulse job at all, rather the sign for a wristwatch like this one." He pulled his uniform jacket sleeve back three inches to reveal a handsome watch. Of course, Lady Darriby-Jones had seen wristwatches before, although she had never purchased one. Indeed, she didn't own any form of watch, whether wrist or pocket, believing there would always be a gentleman on hand if she needed to know the precise time. "They're all the rage at school, auntie," he said.

"Where did you get yours from?" As soon as Lady Darriby-Jones asked that question, she knew it was a mistake and wished, as well as mechanisms to tell the time, there was one to wind back time so mistakes, particularly clumsy questions from aunts, could be undone.

"Mother and father," was all he said, but Lady Darriby-Jones, looking keenly, could see the tears in his eyes, the tautness across his fresh and freckled face. She almost commented on him having the famous Blythe complexion (otherwise known as freckles galore), but stopped herself just in time; that too would be a mistake.

Instead, she turned things to the intensely practical.

"Did you do that essay you were supposed to do over the hols, Freddie?"

"Not yet, but I've given it a lot of thought, aunty."

"Won't you have to turn it in when you get there tonight?"

"Yep, but will do it on the train. Bellamy says that's what the train journey to school is all about. Farringdon says it's a blessing our school is so far away, up north of Inverness, because it gives us bags of time to catch up on stuff like that."

"And what does Freddie Blythe say?" Despite over twenty years rubbing shoulders with the upper class, Lady Darriby-Jones couldn't bring herself to using just surnames for people she was fond of; the one exception was her husband, who she often called just plain, 'Darriby' or 'dear Darriby', depending on various factors including her mood at the time. In fact, she had gone a big step further in recent months, driven by that delightful settling down into middle-aged fondness; now, as often as not, it was, 'Darriby darling', a lovely expression that seemed to sum up both his eccentricities and her regard for the man in two short words.

Freddie had no such reversion to the use of surnames, having been born into the sect. Hence, he told his aunt that, "Blythe would say, thank the spotted cow and all her calves for a long train journey to the Highlands, because it gives one time to get the swots to do the bothersome essay for one."

"And will you pay the swots to do your homework?"

"Yes, aunty, there's a going rate."

"How much?" She was interested to know. In fact, she would love to be a fly in the train compartment while the bunch of schoolboys headed north for the start of term. Well, perhaps not a fly on the wall, because she suspected that, between them, a half-dozen boys could muster some pretty fierce swotting power with whatever exercise books of comic books came to hand.

"Oh, I'd say two slices of Mrs Stone's lovely chocy cake, wouldn't you?"

A little later, as Smith negotiated the narrow lanes through numerous villages on the way to Oxford, Freddie cleared his

The Mystery of the Murder that Wasn't

throat and then introduced the tricky subject of pocket money.

"Mother used to give me ten bob in the first half and the same again in the second half." The way Freddie related many things to a rugger match struck Lady Darriby-Jones; she wondered whether they had oranges at half term and then changed ends when they returned to school.

"I'll match your mama," Lady Darriby-Jones said, feeling an incredible sorrow sweep over her. If she felt this way about a second cousin, once removed and by marriage twice over (the countess' marriage to the earl to bring her into the family and her marriage to Lord Darriby so that she counted as one of the species too), just think what young Freddie was going through. One minute both parents were there, no doubt causing endless embarrassment to young Freddie, his father by shouting too much at rugger matches and his mother by kissing Freddie in public, then the next minute, they were no longer.

Lady Darriby-Jones didn't know too much about events behind the demise of the Earl and Countess of Cosforth, Cosforth being a remote peninsula sticking out into the sea somewhere just above Invergordon.

She had been too tied up in trying to solve the Mystery of the Polite Man last summer, right there at Darriby, to take it all in. But the moment she met Freddie Blythe (Lord Darriby's ward following the death of both parents) at the Christmas half term in late October, she knew he was special and she felt an enormous bond.

Perhaps, with endless January and February stretching out before her, she would do some research and find out what actually went on. Maybe, she would even go to the library today in Oxford and research old papers from last summer, see what she could pick up.

All she knew right then was that they had never found the bodies. That's why young Freddie was not yet termed the Earl of Cosforth; she understood a decent period of time had to pass before that honour was bestowed.

Countryside gave way to suburbia and then suburbia gave way to city centre. She was spending the day in Oxford, a visit to her optician, the one Lady Alice, her daughter, had forced her to go to and she, in return, had taken Ali back to. Alice had been furious to be fitted with the thickest pair of spectacles ever, and had not spoken to her mother for over a week. But she had stopped knocking things over and tripping numerous times a day. Then, Alfie Burrows, Darriby's personal secretary, selected by Lady Darriby-Jones and counted now as a cross between employee and friend, had done a fantastic thing.

"You look so splendid with your glasses on," he had said one breakfast time when she was evidently struggling to read the headlines minus her spectacles, "so intellectual."

Lady Alice had glared back at him, exactly as one would expect from this fiery nineteen-year-old, muttering something about people minding their own business, especially the 'hired help'.

But she had taken to wearing her glasses all the time after that and that's precisely the point from which her record of smashed vases and bruised shins had improved significantly.

After the visit to the optician, Lady Darriby-Jones planned some shopping and had booked a table at Francino's, a favourite restaurant, inviting an old friend she hadn't seen for a number of years. They were going to an afternoon performance of sketches from opera, ambitiously to be performed outside regardless of the weather.

Only, Lady Darriby-Jones, when sending off the sponsorship cheque, had insisted that there be an inside, bad-weather alternative.

All in all, it promised to be a pleasant day. Although she wasn't looking forward to saying goodbye to young Freddie.

The actual goodbye was terribly rushed because of their late start while Freddie made his farewell, 'see you at half-term' rounds of the entire household staff. They almost missed the train to London, where Freddie would change and get the school train from Kings Cross. Smith was sent ahead and he had to call out to make the train wait while Freddie rushed along the platform to the first-class compartments.

No Freddie until half-term. Lady Darriby-Jones reflected for a moment or two on how much she would miss the lively lad, then got on with her busy and enjoyable day, while Smith took the Rolls over to his mother's cottage to catch up with her. Mrs Smith had been the cook at Darriby and a fine, if plain, one she had been. Their lives had changed enormously when she had retired and Mrs Stone had taken over some eight years ago, just as Darriby had come back from the army. His famous statement had been, "so this is how the civvies have been having it while we army bods have survived on rats followed by more rats."

All these thoughts passed through a contended mind as Lady Darriby-Jones sat in the back and Smith trundled through the lanes on their way back to Darriby Hall.

Only to find her home in an uproar. Torino, their Italian butler, was standing on the front steps looking out eagerly for Lady Darriby-Jones.

"Oh, milady," he said, "calamita, calamita, Mr Frederick is mancante, si, si." When the stress level rose, Torino reverted to his native tongue, luckily Lady Darriby-Jones had mastered the basics during their honeymoon when they had first met Torino.

"He's missing? What do you mean?"

Eventually, with the help of Alfie, she got the full story. Freddie had got on the train at Kings Cross, but had not got off at Inverness, for onward travel by bus to Auchin, the tiny village where Freddie's school was situated.

"Lady Darriby-Jones," Alfie added, "what prompted all this was the school calling a few minutes ago to ask why Freddie wasn't on the train."

"But he was. You just said he got on at Kings Cross."

"Yes, but somewhere along the line, he disappeared completely."

Lady Darriby-Jones felt the need for support at such dreadful news. She asked Torino to get a message to Smith that he might be required for extra duty, then retired to the library, where she allowed Alfie to pour each of them a stiff pink gin.

How could a schoolboy vanish from the school train? She would need to investigate.

And pretty presto, to use her Italian.

Chapter Two

There was nothing for it but to drive. If it had been a few hours earlier that she received the news, she could have got the night train to Inverness, but it was already late and they wouldn't get to London in time.

Alfie confirmed this when he found an old timetable from 1921 and it gave the time by train from London to Inverness as ten hours and twenty-two minutes, but the fastest train didn't leave until 10am, a full twelve hours from now.

"If my friend hadn't insisted on dragging me around that dreadful museum," Lady Darriby-Jones said, "I could have got down for the night train up to Inverness and be in Auchin by…" Lady Darriby-Jones had never seen the value in obsessing about the past; it was done and gone, so why worry about dates and history books?

"I think in time for elevenses," Alfie said, flicking through the timetable, "at least in 1921 that was the case."

If Lady Darriby-Jones did not understand the fascination of the past, she also wasn't one to dwell on regrets; what had happened had happened. She couldn't make the train turn around and come back for her, so there was nothing for it but to make a new plan.

A plan that, inevitably, involved Smith, particularly as she wasn't aware that anybody else could manage a motor car. She had tried several times on the drive, but the car hadn't behaved itself and had shuddered to a violent stop each time.

In any long-distance race to the north, she would provide the moral support rather than take a turn at the wheel.

"Could you come with me, Alfie?" she asked, thinking the more people able to prop Smith's eyes open with matchsticks, the better.

"I'm sorry, Lady Darriby-Jones. I have an important meeting tomorrow morning with the Slug Council of Great Britain. We're hosting them here, as you were probably aware, following the magnificent success of the symposium last year."

"Yes, of course, I quite forgot." Alfie had been recruited by her last summer when a series of private secretaries had disappeared down the drive concerned at Darriby's request to cut up slugs and get involved in areas they were too squeamish to be happy about.

She had gone to Oxford and had stumbled into Alfie Burrows at just the right moment. He had just been let go from a menswear shop. She forgot the name, because of a propensity to borrow the expensive suits and hats and wear them on his days' off. He had become the perfect secretary to Lord Darriby-Jones.

But Lady Darriby-Jones wished she could lay claim to him as he was everything she could wish for in an assistant, even sharing her taste in pink gin.

"But I believe Lady Alice is free if you need some company," Alfie said, meaning it to be helpful. However, the thought of twelve or fourteen hours closeted in a little Rolls Royce with her only daughter, was too much for her and she declined the suggestion, saying she was sure Smith would cope very well with a few breaks for coffee now and then.

Smith, summoned by Torino, arrived at that very moment. Lady Darriby-Jones had to think quickly and imaginatively. It was a lot to ask of a man, to motor over five-hundred miles through the night after a full day ferrying her around. She needed an enticement and then she remembered.

"Ah, Smith," she said, as if she had happened upon him in the hallway, rather than him being summoned urgently, "I have good news and bad news. Which will you have first?"

"Oh, always the bad first, milady. Things can only get better then, you see?"

"So be it, Smith. I have need of your services again right now."

Well, the expression on Smith's face said he had gotten off lightly; he probably imagined a trip out to pick someone up at Oxford because they had missed the last train to Darriby Halt.

"Of course, milady. Where to?" And there was still the good news to come.

"Auchin."

"Where's that, milady? This side of Oxford or the other?"

"Oh, it's decidedly the other side of Oxford. I believe it's about five-hundred miles the other side. Alfie, please be so kind as to show Smith the map. I need to get there sooner than soon, if you get my meaning."

"Scotland? But you never drive to Scotland, milady. You always take the train. I take the car up and stop by my cousins for a few days on the way up and down, break the journey, like."

"Not this time, Smith. I need maximum speed up the north road. You see, Freddie has disappeared and we have to find him."

"Of course, milady." Everyone liked Freddie enormously, it being a physical impossibility to dislike the boy. You could be angry with him, sick and tired of his cheery cheekiness, but never to the extent of wishing him anything but the very best. "Is he alright, milady?"

"We really don't know, Smith. His disappearance is a complete mystery to us all." And that brought to mind the good news, which Lady Darriby-Jones hurried to rattle out. "The good news is that there's every chance that you could be involved in a new mystery, Smith, every chance indeed."

After Smith left to get ready, Lady Darriby-Jones wondered briefly why Smith had not taken the good news so well; did not everyone relish mysteries and the solving of them? Was that not a main plank of life, especially in rural northwest Oxfordshire, where nothing much changed year on year?

"Torino, we'll need plenty of coffee and sandwiches for the trip."

"Yes, milady, I'll make up a basket. We have two of those new-fangled vacuum flasks we can use to keep the coffee hot." They weren't that new-fangled, having been around a few decades, but Torino delighted in his misinterpretation of being English, including a disdain for anything not invented or discovered at least two generations earlier.

They set off half-an-hour later, after Tilly had packed a suitcase and loaded it in the back. Mrs Smith clearly did the same for her husband and both suitcases fitted nicely.

"No, Torino. I'll go in the front to keep Smith company as he has many hours ahead of him."

"Are you sure, milady?" Smith asked, not sure if he wanted the company of his employer.

"Yes, I'm determined to keep you awake, Smith. I might even sing opera to you to do so."

"Yes, milady, thank you, milady." He couldn't stand opera and couldn't see the fuss of it, lots of shrieking from people who would do well as supporters at a football match.

Lady Darriby-Jones was good to her word on the great trip north. She started by playing a game of seeing every letter of the alphabet on number plates. The fact that they were driving at night meant there were precious few and they reached Manchester before they had been twice around the alphabet.

They stopped for a 'midnight feast' at the side of the road at some desolate part of Lancashire. In the summer, it would be early morning with the sun leaning over the Pennines and waking up the sleepy towns and villages of Lancs.

In early January, it was pitch black and raining hard.

Lady Darriby-Jones tried a little opera after the first break for coffee, but quickly noticed that Smith had an aversion to it, such that he wobbled across the road as he tried to block out the sound with his hands.

They stopped again just south of Glasgow. They had some breakfast in an inn by the side of the road, run by a dour Glaswegian who grumbled when Lady Darriby-Jones insisted that Smith get the same breakfast as her rather than eating with the staff in the kitchen. By now it was daylight, if it could be called that. The grey to black clouds hung low in the sky like a suspended ceiling. The ground had patches of snow, giving it an irregular checked look, as if God above had flicked paint from giant paintbrushes, perhaps after a session painting the future of the world. And then there was the wind, constant and cold, so Lady Darriby-Jones was pleased to hurry back to the car and tuck a warm rug around her.

They still had the Cairngorms to get through and then on to the Grampians where she believed Auchin lay nestled in a glen that led steeply down from the mountains all around.

Somehow, they made it by lunchtime. Lady Darriby-Jones asked Smith to drop her at the school, find a suitable hotel and get a couple of hours of kip before collecting her a little later on.

She walked into the school and was met by sounds and sights she knew from Lady Alice's brief experiment with boarding school, but had never experienced herself. Her own schooling having been extremely patchy.

She asked for the headmaster and was shown in a pleasant sitting room in which every spare bit of wall contained pictures of sports teams, all with the surnames of the individual team members marked below, some with designations such as 'minor' or 'major'.

"What do you do when there are three brothers?" she asked the secretary, who brought a cup of coffee.

"What do you mean?"

"Well, you have minor and major, but what of the middle one?" The secretary looked blankly at her and then fell back on the standard.

"Mr Hardway will be with you in a moment, Lady Darriby-Jones."

"Not Major Blythe?" For a moment, she thought she was being palmed off with a deputy, but the secretary explained that Major Blythe, Freddie's uncle, had retired just over a year ago and Mr Hardway had taken over.

Mr Hardway was the type you heard before you saw. Loud noises, that could be English or could, equally, be some foreign language, came in to the relative silence of the waiting room from some distance away. As they moved closer, she could make out some of the words.

"Get Turpin, damn you. He needs to report to Lady Darriby-Jones pronto. Well, wake the bugger up, damn him. I don't care if he's been up half the bloody night."

It was schoolboy language, yet coming from the headmaster, who she had yet to set eyes on.

When she did, her only response was a sharp intake of breath. He seemed the very archetypical school bully, yet was strangely dressed in a kilt with a mortar board. His face was ruddy and fleshy, with the tiniest eyes and fattest lips she had ever seen; clearly not the finest specimen of a human being, especially as a considerable amount of flab hung from his frame like ill-fitting curtains.

"Hardway, Ian, Headmaster for my sins."

Lady Darriby-Jones was tempted to reply in similar manner but didn't, concerned that, unpractised at turning names on their head, she would get the order completely wrong and appear foolish.

"I'm a MacGregor, that's my clan," he announced, indicating a weakness many Englishmen living in Scotland suffer from, a need to associate themselves with Highland links in some way or other.

Hardway was quite clearly not Scottish but was trying incredibly hard to be so.

Mr Turpin followed after a few minutes of embarrassed and disjointed conversation between the two of them, the type that never really gets going.

"Ah Turpin, Lady Darriby-Jones would like you to recount to her what you told me yesterday evening when young Blythe failed to report for duty. Over to you, Turpin."

The Mystery of the Murder that Wasn't

Mr Turpin, clearly recently roused from his bed, swallowed hard a couple of times before launching into his story. And what Lady Darriby-Jones heard left her astounded that Auchin School for Boys was permitted to look after a monkey, let alone three-hundred adolescent boys.

Chapter Three

"You see, it was like this..."

Lady Darriby-Jones had been around for a while, although she still counted herself very much on the youthful side of the watershed. She knew from experience that anyone who started a conversation in the way Mr Turpin had was trying to explain away their own inadequacies, and this time was no exception.

"Let me get this right," she said at the first break she could manage into his monotone, "you were in the station bar at Kings Cross right up until the last minute before the train went?"

"That's right, lady, eh..."

"The correct title is Lady Darriby-Jones, damn you, Turpin." That was Hardway, not Lady Darriby-Jones at all.

"And who checked off the boys against the list?"

"Ah, well, that's traditionally the responsibility of the head boy or the senior prefect."

"So, you weren't involved?"

"No... Lady Darriby-Jones. They presented the list to me and said everyone was on board."

"Did you check the list?"

"I didn't... eh... see a need to, Lady Darriby-Jones."

"How many stops between Kings Cross and Inverness?" That threw Turpin; he clearly had no idea, having slept through the entire journey. "No matter, I'll ask at Auchin station when I go there." She was already disgusted with Turpin's responses and, knowing he would be no good to the cause of finding Freddie, wanted to get him out of there as soon as possible. "Was anyone else missing when you or the head boy or whoever checked the list again when boarding the buses at Inverness station?"

"No, just Blythe, only he was missing."

"Thank you, Mr Turpin." The door opened and the door closed. Between those two actions, there was an amount of shuffling as the sorry figure of Turpin, teacher of Religious Education and Ancient History, and, inevitably, a big target of the boys' jokes, was gone.

"He's for the bloody high jump," Hardway said just before the door closed, calculated to ensure that Turpin would hear.

"Can your secretary organise a telegram?" Lady Darriby-Jones was moving on, no point in trying to graze on barren land.

"Certainly," he replied, then bellowed some name she could not catch. The secretary was clearly frightened of Hardway; ten or fifteen years earlier, she would have been the same.

The telegram went to Darriby Hall and read:

> *In Auchin. Stop. Need Alfie and Alice. Stop. Suggest night train tonight. Stop. Confirm travel arrangements. Stop.*

She always loved sending and receiving telegrams, liking the abbreviated sentences and the 'stops' between.

"Right," she said, "that's that done. I'm going to wait downstairs for my chauffeur and will be back in the morning when I'd like to interview the boys in his carriage."

"Righto, Lady Darriby-Jones, have someone attend, make sure boys on their best..." He sounded like a walking telegram himself.

Some timings work out and some do not. As Lady Darriby-Jones walked out into the surprising sunshine of a late January afternoon in the Highlands, Smith drove in up the long drive to the school and came to park at the front door the very moment Lady Darriby-Jones reached the bottom of the steps. He hopped out and held the door for her.

"Where to?" she said.

"The Auchin Hotel," he replied, "it's actually the only place around." When they were in the car, with Lady Darriby-Jones back in the rear seat, he spoke through the voice pipe to say not to expect luxury as the hotel was pretty basic.

At least it wasn't a long drive. In fact, it could be walked in under ten minutes. The buildings of Auchin village were all a type of grey stone she imagined was quarried locally and therefore cheap to buy because no need to transport them far. They didn't have a lot to recommend them. The Auchin Hotel was no different, just larger with two bars downstairs and a tiny restaurant built as a conservatory on the back. They were met by the oddest of girls, probably in her early twenties, with jet black hair and bright green eyes.

"This is Lady Darriby-Jones," Smith introduced her.

"Welcome to the forgotten corner of Scotland," the girl replied, although Lady Darriby-Jones couldn't imagine how a steep glen could be a corner. "What brings you here?"

"Oh, school business. My relative is in attendance."

"Not young Mr Blythe? He mentioned that, with his parents dead, he was going to stay with you."

"Yes, that's right. Do you know him?"

"We're good friends, I suppose. You see, I work part time in the accounts office at the school. He's more fun than all the other boys put together, I'd say. I'm Cathy MacIntyre, the daughter of the landlord and landlady."

"Do you know where he is?"

"Why, at school, of course. Term started yesterday. I believe the exams start tomorrow." Whenever Lady Darriby-Jones heard about exams starting, she offered up a silent prayer that she had never had to take an exam in her life. It seemed so unfair to put that burden on mere children, also, to have them right after the Christmas hols was downright killjoy.

The Mystery of the Murder that Wasn't

When Lady Darriby-Jones told the girl about Freddie's disappearance, she grew very serious and said she had been expecting it.

"What on earth do you mean?"

"Well, sort of expecting it. You see, Freddie and I went to see a fortune teller last term. One Saturday he pretended to have hurt his knee to get off games and we got a lift together into Invergordon. We saw this lady who told us things."

"What?" then followed up with, "What did she say?"

"Just that there will be a grand reunion for the young man and I said, that's easy because everyone will meet up again in Heaven, unless, of course, they've been really bad and she just looked at me and said the reunion will be sooner than that, much sooner."

"When did you last see Freddie?"

"Oh, the last day of term, I think it was, back before Christmas. I was planning to sneak into the playground and see him tomorrow, but now you say he's not there."

That night, in her dream, in an uncomfortable bed in a strange room, she put a pointed hat on Cathy MacIntyre and saw her fully as a witch. It could have just been the way the night light on the landing placed shadows in her room, but she woke certain that Cathy was a witch.

Not that she really believed in witches, but you never know.

. . .

The morning was very different with bright sunshine and a light breeze. Smith trundled the car back to the school and Lady Darriby-Jones presented herself for the interviews.

Five boys were marched into the same sitting room, led by Mrs Botham, the matron. She had heard Freddie refer to her as 'Old Ma Bosom' and could see why; her chest was enormous, think of a number and double it. Then you'll be getting somewhere reasonably close. She wore what was probably the largest matron uniform ever made, but still it was tight. Moreover, she was below average height and her uniform dress hung almost to her ankles.

She did have a cheery smile and a way with the boys; they clearly adored her.

"I've put them in alphabetical order," she said after taking Lady Darriby-Jones' offered hand, but doing a mini curtsey at the same time. "Shall I shoo then out and let one in at a time?"

"Yes, that would be fine." In truth, Lady Darriby-Jones had no plan for carrying out the investigation into the missing boy, rather like a sail-torn boat limping across the sea, she would take what current and wind she could find.

Bellew came first, a tall lanky kid with a funny smirk that made you think he took pleasure in other people's misfortunes. He had been growing too fast for the school outfitters, leaving his shins on display with a good six inches showing.

He knew little about Freddie's disappearance, saying the train had stopped at several places like York and Newcastle and Durham and some other places he couldn't remember, then declaring that he had been out of the carriage most of the time, pleading with Forster to do his blasted essay.

"The brat wanted to charge two shillings, don't you know?"

"When did you last see Freddie?"

"Who? Oh, you mean Blythe. Well, I dunno, probably not too long after we left London, I 'spect he was looking for someone to do his essay too."

Next came Carter, and Lady Darriby-Jones took an instant dislike when the first words he uttered were to ask about a reward. He wanted to sell his information and Lady Darriby-Jones passed over half a crown before realising that he knew even less than Bellew. She dismissed him quickly with a brisk thanks for his trouble and an even brisker 'next'.

Number three was a quiet lad called Davies, who spoke in a permanent whisper. He claimed in hush-hush tones that Blythe was part of a criminal gang involved in importing weapons to start a revolution, "just like in Russia". Old Ma Bosom interrupted to explain that Davies' nickname at school was Trotsky because he was always one to vote for revolution, "if you can vote for revolution, that is, which I rather think you can't."

"When did you last see Blythe?" Lady Darriby-Jones asked Davies, thinking to bring him back to ground if she could.

But no joy; instead, Davies span a long yarn about boys from another carriage pulling an ever-increasing array of nasty weapons.

"No doubt," he whispered, "the other carriage took him away." That's when Old Ma thought it best to advise Lady Darriby-Jones that they boys rushed onto the school train to bag carriages and then guarded them fiercely against attacks from other compartments throughout the journey, "it's like the Somme on that train," she laughed, "I should know, because I was there."

Lady Darriby-Jones was left wondering about the moral effect of presenting the biggest bosoms ever encased in a nurse's uniform to a bunch of wounded soldiers; clearly, someone had done something right during that disastrous and dreadful war.

Phillips Major came next. He, at least, could confirm that Blythe was in his seat when the train left Edinburgh station.

"I sat oppo Blythe and the prefects don't let us out of our seats in stations."

"Why's that, Phillips?"

"Because we go onto the platform for tuck and last term someone got stranded at the station when the train pulled out. No, Blythe was defo there as the train chugged out of Edinburgh. Then the aliens came in, like squeezing their wispy bodies through that little window that really opens, whereas the others are just pretend."

"Who's pretending?" Lady Darriby-Jones was finding it hard to keep up.

"The windows, of course, but they may have been ghosts, come to think of it. Not the windows but the aliens."

That's the point at which Lady Darriby-Jones gave up.

The final boy was Wilson Minor, a much more thoughtful character. He was younger than the others, who were all around Freddie's age. He was only included, so Old Ma Bosom told her, because Wilson Minor was Phillips Major's great uncle.

"What? Surely not?"

"True as the day I was born," Old Ma Bosom said, "somewhere along the way the Phillips branch slipped two whole generations. I think it was probably carelessness."

As Lady Darriby-Jones spent more time with Old Ma Bosom, she realised the worst crime in the matron's book was being careless.

Put a murderer next to a clumsy boy and she would sit up half the night remonstrating with the clumsy boy.

Wilson Minor was able to confirm that Blythe had been on the train at least as far as Edinburgh. He had seen Blythe as the train pulled into Stirling station, but had not seen him after it had moved away again.

. . .

"That narrows it down, considerably," she said as she got back into the car to go and meet the others at Inverness station. "My money's on the fact that he was snatched at Stirling station. The next big question is why would anyone want to kidnap a schoolboy?"

Chapter Four

Tension can be visible. Other times, it hides itself away only to spring out suddenly and surprise all around who had assumed, quite naturally, that everything was alright.

Not now, not as the train pulled into the station and the porters rushed to the first-class carriages in the hope of obtaining a large tip. Lady Darriby-Jones actually felt the tension in the air as she waited for her two passengers to alight.

Lady Darriby-Jones didn't rush at all. Rushing would lack dignity; besides, she didn't feel like charging all over the place, still suffering from the long journey by motor car, virtually the whole length of the island they called home. She moved at a nice, even and moderate pace, logically towards the first-class carriages. Smith fell in to a respectful towed position behind her.

There they waited, slap bang in the middle of the two first-class carriages.

"Hello, Lady Darriby-Jones." She turned around, spinning on a sixpence, or almost achieving that feat at any rate.

"Where... how... I mean..."

"We just got off the train," Alfie said.

"Mr Burrows insisted on going second-class," Lady Alice said, "making it the worst journey in the records of human journeys."

"Worse than Magellan's circumnavigation of the world?" Alfie wanted to know.

"Maggie who?"

"Magellan, not Maggie. He was a mister, for your information. Their journey was, you know, eating rats and the like, dying of scurvy left, right and centre."

That was the tension, sitting up at the caustic words the two new arrivals shared between themselves.

Clearly, it hadn't been a happy journey. And, it would seem, for no other reason than Alfie's decision to go second-class, with all the associated inconveniences that the saving of a fistful of coins had entailed.

Not that Lady Darriby-Jones had ever gone second-class, but that was by the by.

"Let's get everyone back to the hotel and then we can sort out somewhere to eat," Lady Darriby-Jones said.

"Actually, milady, there's only the hotel to eat in. That's the only restaurant for miles around, so I'm informed." Smith knew that the only proper time to interject anything into this conversation was through the polite correction of facts, such as the density and quality of eating establishments in the area.

"Well, then, the hotel it will be."

They piled into the car and Smith drove at a sedate pace over to Auchin and the little glen where it laid.

"So, let me get this straight, if you'd be so kind, Lady Darriby-Jones," Alfie said into the expired exuberance that itself was quickly fading. "Freddie has done a runner..."

"Or they've nipped him, probably for a fat ransom."

"Yes, that's a distinct possibility, Lady Alice. We do have to consider all options, of course." This was all daggers drawn stuff. Who would survive to tell the tale? She didn't want Alfie and Ali to be in a state of fisticuffs; she liked them a lot.

She genuinely warmed to Alfie and loved her daughter, although nobody could get that close to her.

"Have you contacted the police, Lady Darriby-Jones?" Alfie asked.

"Of course, mother has contacted the police," Lady Alice replied before seeking confirmation from Lady Darriby-Jones, a big mistake.

"Actually, I haven't yet. I really didn't think about doing so, at least not until I had a few facts to back up my case."

Lady Alice responded with a loud snort and turned her head directly away from the others to stare out of the window at nothing at all.

"Don't you think...?" Alfie seemed to have moved beyond the petty fighting with Lady Alice, now applying common sense to a tricky situation. Lady Darriby-Jones knew him well enough to see that he was gently challenging her reluctance to trust the police; who wouldn't after her experiences with the local Darriby force?

But, he had a point. What if Freddie had been kidnapped or, worse still, was lying somewhere in a ditch, bound and gagged and slowly dying without any chance of rescue?

"We'll go right now, then. You're right Alfie, my dear." That was met with another snort as Lady Alice's head turned even further away from the others.

The police station was the same grey stone as the rest of the buildings in Auchin, same grey slate on the roof, too. Lady Darriby-Jones wondered if some local ordnance dictated that all buildings be constructed out of shades of grey, no colour allowed.

Inside, however, it was much brighter. A fire roared in the grate in the main office and an oversized policeman asked politely what he could do to help them.

"We need to report a missing person," Alfie said. "Lady Darriby-Jones has the details."

Five minutes later, they were in the inspector's office, sipping tea and discussing the case with Inspector MacBride, a genial man who obviously ran a genial station.

"Can you please give me the boy's name again?" he said, his pencil end in his mouth, wagging up and down as he spoke. He, too, seemed oversized, making Lady Darriby-Jones wonder if you needed to be near giant status to get accepted into the Highland Constabulary.

"It's the Honourable Frederick Blythe, born on the 10th October 1910 and currently a pupil at Auchin School for Boys, although not currently, in that he didn't turn up the day before yesterday for the start of term."

A series of questions followed concerning when he was last seen, the mode of travel, whether he had any enemies or anyone who had it in for him. Lady Darriby-Jones answered them all, explaining that their best guess was that he had been snatched off the train at Stirling station.

"No doubt he's lying tied up in some deserted warehouse with rats crawling all over him," Lady Alice added, although she had no basis for this assertion.

"Can you leave it with me a moment?" Inspector MacBride said, "we'll have to liaise with other police forces along the track as it were."

"Yes, of course, inspector," Lady Darriby-Jones replied, actually pleasantly surprised not to have the mixture of aggression and sarcasm she could count on receiving from DCI 'Bad' Manners back home. Perhaps they taught you how to be a gentleman in other forces. She would have to mention her experiences to the Chief Constable when she next saw him.

"Bullock will take some further details," the Inspector said, "no need to leave my office, Bullock will come in here."

Bullock turned out to be WPC Sandra Bullock, a gorgeous female police officer with a personality to match. Lady Darriby-Jones noted Lady Alice turning in her chair once again, evidently feeling she couldn't face Alfie making eyes with a pretty and alluring officer of the law in her smart uniform that, she noticed, didn't preclude a little makeup and nail varnish.

If Alice turned any more in her chair, she thought, she would be right back to facing the front again and then what would she do?

Sandra Bullock was also a rapid notetaker, scribbling furiously all the details Alfie gave about Freddie's family, engrossed in the process, while Alice sat fuming and shunting her chair this way and that.

Inspector MacBride returned to the office after a brief conflab with Bullock in the corridor. Each time they said something, Lady Darriby-Jones could see the other look at her through the open doorway.

Something wasn't going right. In fact, it was going decidedly wrong.

When the inspector finally made it back into his own office, even Lady Alice turned in her chair to face him.

"I'm afraid I've got some rather bad news for you," he said. "Well, I suppose it's bad news tinged with good, although you might well argue that it's good news tinged with bad."

"What is it, Inspector?"

"We know exactly where your nephew is, Lady Darriby-Jones, and he's not been kidnapped by aliens or ghosts of Russians, or anyone else for that matter." He paused for a second. Lady Darriby-Jones sensed the crunch line was coming. In fact, she felt it directed straight for her.

"Where is he?" she asked in a significantly weaker voice than was her norm. Lady Darriby-Jones fitted the category of bellower rather than titterer, usually, but not now, not in Auchin police station in a comfy room in a comfy station of what looked to be a decidedly uncomfortable looking village.

Looks can be deceiving.

"We know these things, Lady Darriby-Jones, because Blythe, Frederick, the Honourable, is currently in police custody."

"Police custody? The boy wouldn't hurt a fly." That was Lady Alice, completely back in the frame now, livid that someone had done this to her second cousin twice removed or third cousin once removed, or whatever the exact relationship was.

"I assure you, Lady Alice, it is absolutely correct. He's being held in Stirling pending transfer to court and then remand the moment the charges are brought forward."

"What are the charges?" Lady Darriby-Jones heard herself saying the words, but had no recollection of putting them out there.

"Why, it's murder of course. He's accused of killing both his mother and his father, they being the Earl and Countess of Cosforth, who happen to be big fish to fry, around here at any rate."

Chapter Five

"Very big fish to fry," Lady Darriby-Jones said. "In fact, poor Freddie is being fried when he hasn't got a malicious bone in his body."

"Unfortunately, mother, the law doesn't work like that."

"Like what?" Lady Darriby-Jones felt the same sweep of helplessness as mothers feel when their youngsters go missing. She hadn't known Freddie terribly well before his parents had died, but had got to know him in super quick time since then. One Christmas hols and a half-term before that and he had endeared himself to the whole cast that strutted the Darriby stage.

Her included, without a doubt.

"The law deals in facts, not impressions, mother."

"What does?" Her world was closing in, all reason opting out of work mode; Lady Darriby-Jones couldn't make sense of anything whatsoever.

If Freddie was a criminal, then not only could pigs fly but they could walk on their hind legs and talk the talk to convince everyone they were slightly pinker than usual humans.

Her thoughts weren't making any sense at all.

Get a grip, Lady Darriby-Jones

That was it. Get a grip. She took a deep breath, then a turn around the police station for some air. She slowed her breathing, deepening it instead. Finally, she went back indoors, feeling somewhat straightened out.

"Inspector MacBride," she started, "I would beg a little more of your time, please."

"I tell you what, Lady Darriby-Jones, I've read up on this case quite a lot over the last half an hour. I'm off duty in a moment."

"Oh well, at least please give me something to go with before you go off."

"I was going to suggest that you come around to our place. It's not grand like I imagine Darriby Hall to be, but it's our home and you're very welcome there."

"But that would be an imposition on you and on Mrs MacBride, if there is a Mrs MacBride, that is."

"Nonsense, nonsense, nonsense. Why, only this morning Mrs McB, that's my lovely other half by the way, was saying that nothing exciting ever happens around here. It would be lovely to bring a real humdinger of a mystery home to let her work her grey cells on."

The Mystery of the Murder that Wasn't

Mention of the word 'grey' made Lady Darriby-Jones think of grey people with grey cells working in grey environments. She thought back to the school. She had thought Freddie was very smart in his uniform with blazer, cap and tie. Yet, the uniform was almost entirely grey, just little splashes of colour in the ties and caps.

Then she realised that her mind was drifting again, circling around the facts like a vulture around a carcase, yet the kind inspector was waiting for an answer to his offer of domestic bliss and criminal explanation combined.

"Yes, inspector, we would love to come to your house, but there are four of us, because we have Smith, the chauffeur sitting outside in the car."

"Well, there's four of us, too. Mrs McB, myself and our two bairns, except they're halfway to being grown boys now. Actually, if it's not too cheeky to ask?"

"What's that, inspector?"

"Well, if your chauffeur was willing to take the boys for a spin in your car, I'm sure they would adore it."

"Done deal," Lady Darriby-Jones replied with a smile, "done deal."

The package included 'tea' which actually consisted of fish and chips collected by Smith and the two MacB boys in the Rolls, including a twenty-minute detour on the way to the chippie in which Smith put the car through its paces.

This gave time for five people to gather around the tiny kitchen table while the inspector announced that he had brought a real humdinger of a mystery home, "just for you, Mrs MacB."

"That's very kind of you, Mr MacB," came the reply in the thickest Scottish accent she had ever heard after twenty highly enjoyable autumns on their Scottish estate.

Just never quite this far north, so maybe that explained it.

"Right," Lady Alice seemed to be over her big sulk, although she still didn't sit anywhere near Alfie, "let's get some order into this. Remind me, everyone, what the agenda is."

"Quite simple, Ali dear, we want to know all known facts about the Cosforth murders."

"Alright, I'll begin," the inspector said.

He did begin then and held the audience spellbound until the end, a perfect storyteller in every regard.

Forgive my ignorance as to certain details, I've only recently become acquainted with the Cosford Case. There are two facts of considerable interest in this case and I want to dwell a moment on each one.

The first is that this is a no-body murder. I don't mean that nobody has been murdered, or that the person or people murdered were nobodies. Two people do appear to have been killed, namely the Earl and Countess of Cosforth, your Freddie's parents and certainly people of note around here. I mean that no bodies have been found.

It might seem odd to have a murder without a body but, rest assured, it does happen from time to time. There are usually

The Mystery of the Murder that Wasn't

particular circumstances when a murder investigation is started without a body to put the fact of murder beyond doubt. One of those cases concerns close family members who disappear. So, first established fact; it's possible to have a murder without a body. Full stop, as in I mean what I say.

Second fact coming up now and this concerns supporting evidence, often vital in cases like these. We have some letters, rather dark letters, I'm afraid to say and, surprisingly, made public in an extraordinary way.

These letters are written by young Freddie and seem to dwell on an extraordinarily morbid subject, that being the intention and the precise planning behind the demise of both parents. That's to say planned, premediated, intended and then carried out by virtue of those parents not being around and able to declare their fitness for this world.

How did these letters come to be known to the police, I imagine you asking? Many such intensely morbid thoughts must be produced every day of the year, yet are kept secret from prying eyes, particularly the prying eyes of the law.

Well, the answer to this question is to be found in the newspaper, but not as a reported news item.

The paper in question is the Highland Encompass, an obscure weekly edition that circulates in and around Inverness. Someone, presumably not Freddie Blythe, sent these letters in to the paper and they were published last week in the first edition of the new year.

There are three letters, ladies and gentleman. They cover, in order, the preparations, the murders and the disposing of the bodies, although, frustratingly, the last letter is much more obscure than the first two, hence we still have not located any bodies.

The letters received many complaints; apparently the graphic detail they go into is beyond most people's idea of common decency. The level of complaint brought the matter to the attention of the Inverness police who then learnt that the Honourable Freddie Blythe would be travelling north on the school train. They deemed there to be risk of bodily harm to Freddie at Inverness station, the earl and countess being popular local figures. Therefore they collaborated with Stirling police and arranged for his detention when the train pulled in there.

He's been transferred up to Inverness police station in an unmarked car and is being held there pending charges. The Inverness police are also trying to determine who sent the letters to the Highland Encompass but the newspaper is not being particularly helpful.

"I see," said Lady Darriby-Jones when the inspector wound up his narrative. What else could she say? It was a bombshell of the first order.

She knew Freddie and she knew he was innocent but every single piece of information led in the opposite direction.

Who else would gain from the death of the earl and countess? Who on earth? She had no idea. By all accounts, they were popular and well-liked.

"It makes for grim conclusions," Lady Alice said.

"Grim indeed," Alfie added, no tension between them evident now; it would seem that events regarding Freddie had blown their petty squabbles out of the window and up the glen.

"There's no way of looking at it," Lady Darriby-Jones concluded, "but that Freddie's in a particularly sticky spot."

Chapter Six

Lady Darriby-Jones was up early the next morning, keen to get on with what little she could do. However, she didn't skip, or skimp on, her breakfast, knowing this to be the foundation stone to her day.

Alfie came down when she was half way through and asked what he could do.

"Eat up quickly and come with me," she replied. "I'll go and shift Lady Alice and we'll all go together."

"Where are we going?" Alfie asked.

"Why, to visit poor Freddie, of course. We've got to buck him up for whatever trails he faces in the near term. Yes, I know it's not perfect, but it's something."

She went back across the bar, now closed, and noticed Cathy looking closely at her with her bright green eyes, a vision complete with witch's hat passing briefly into her mind.

"Any news on Freddie?" Cathy asked.

"Not much," Lady Darriby-Jones lied, then felt bad about it, "just that he's been arrested for the murder of his parents."

"So, he did then? Murder his parents, I mean." It was almost as if Cathy had turned up at the cinema for a date and found the latest movie was showing, the one with her favourite actor; Lady Darriby-Jones had once been to the cinema and could picture the scene.

"I don't think so. In fact, I'm sure it's not the case and he's as innocent as the days are long." Such a strange expression, especially set in mid-winter in the Highlands, when the days were exceptionally short.

She continued across the bar, intent on the stairs to the first floor and the waking of her daughter, then she stopped and turned slowly back towards the bar area where, moments earlier, Cathy had been polishing glasses, making each one shine gloriously.

There was no Cathy there, yet the only way out from behind the bar was into the main room or down into the cellar.

"Cathy?" she called down the cellar steps, no reply, no movement. She found the light switch and went down the steep steps, definitely no one in there, nothing unusual except a high-up window open to the strong wind blowing what must be from ground level outside. The wind made an eerie sound through the window that Lady Darriby-Jones found disturbing.

She retraced her steps and went outside. Nobody. Shrugging, she went back into the hotel and went upstairs to begin the process of waking her daughter.

The Mystery of the Murder that Wasn't

. . .

One thing she liked about Lady Alice, her daughter, was that she had a mind of her own. On entering the school, picking up on those distinctly boarding school smells of wet clothes, mud and cocoa, she said she wouldn't be a minute and slipped off down a side passage which led to who knows where. Alfie stayed resolutely with Lady Darriby-Jones and she couldn't work out whether that was due to the lingering angry dispute over class of travel yesterday, or whether Alfie felt a compulsion to protect her from the blubbery form of Mr Hardway, who she had described in detail over the breakfast time they had shared.

This time, Lady Darriby-Jones and Alfie were taken straight to the headmaster's study, actually a suite of rooms on the first floor overlooking the side of the old mansion in which the school was located, also built of grey stone under grey slates.

The presence of Mr Hardway was, as before, heard before it was seen. Evidentially, in the inner office to the mini complex, there was a row of some sort going on. The secretary, all grey to match the architecture, hesitated to knock on the door, so Lady Darriby-Jones fulfilled that task for her, probably with a lot more gusto than the secretary would have done.

"What the blazes do you want?" came back through the door, all the soft tone of the Scottish accent forgotten in his flaring up.

"It's Lady Darriby-Jones together with my personal secretary and we would like a word, Mr Hardway." She had promoted Alfie in an instant, or moved him sideways depending on your point of view.

The door opened and Mr Turpin scuttled out, as if a rocket had been lit in his underpants.

No doubt, it probably had.

"Come in, come in, Och, it's a sad turn of events is all this." He remembered his Scottish tones and slipped them in again.

He was dressed in his kilt, although Lady Darriby-Jones noted it was a different tartan to yesterday. So much for his allegiance to the MacGregor clan.

"What can I do for you, Lady Darriby-Jones?"

"This is my personal secretary, Mr Burrows." Promotion or sideways move once again. Lady Darriby-Jones noted the slight smile on Alfie's face and took that to be approval. "Mr Hardway, I have grave news concerning young Freddie."

She didn't do the full version of the tale that Inspector MacB had filled them in on the previous evening. That wasn't for this oafish bully of a man to worry about. Instead, she condensed it into the essentials on a hastily put together need to know basis.

"Freddie's being held by the police and we need to get a reference as to his character," she summed up. "We want that to be from you, Mr Hardway."

"Certainly, Lady Darriby-Jones. My secretary will type something up and will send it down to the Auchin Hotel when it's complete, probably first thing in the morning."

"That will be very satisfactory. I'm sure you'll see the benefits of stressing the many excellent parts of his character, Mr Hardway? It will, of course, reflect well on the school, all that character-building stuff that parents like so much."

"I understand entirely, Lady Darriby-Jones. Now, if you'll excuse me, I have urgent need of placing an advertisement for a new RE and Ancient History teacher."

Lady Alice was waiting when they came down the stairs, a young, timid teacher in tow.

"This is Malcolm Robertson," she said, "he's quite new here, was appointed just over a year ago by Freddie's uncle, Major Blythe. He has something to say to you, mother." Lady Alice managed to move so that her back was towards Alfie, blocking him from seeing Mr Robertson with any clarity.

"Good morning, Lady Darriby-Jones. I just wanted to raise some delicate matters concerning probity at the school. You see, there are some funny goings-on and I don't know who else to talk to it about them."

"The governors, perhaps?" Despite her poor education, she was a governor, indeed chairwoman of the board, at Darriby Village School, and had an inkling of the contribution governors made to the smooth and proper running of any school.

"Yes, quite, but that's the rub, you see. Both governors are dead."

"You mean...?"

"Yes, the Earl and Countess of Cosforth. They set up the school and donated the buildings and now with them no longer of this world, there doesn't seem to be any priority in replacing them."

"I see, well can you meet us later at the hotel? Alfie will take notes on the full set of concerns and I'll then make a decision as to what to do."

"Yes, of course, Lady Darriby-Jones. Thank you for your time and I will see you later this evening. Maybe around 8pm when prep is over?"

On the way to the car, Lady Darriby-Jones asked her daughter how she had managed to find Mr Robertson, a teacher who was prepared to stand up to the bully-boy tactics of Mr Hardway.

"Oh, that's simple," she replied. "I just sniffed him out." She added to the joke by making large sniffing noises around her mother. "Let's see what we have here."

"What we have here, Ali dear, is one very concerned aunt who is taking us this moment to see her dear but troubled nephew. All aboard, it seems, for Inverness Police Station."

Which building, surprisingly, was not built of grey stone with grey slates on top. It had been designed by an architect as a modern effort and was actually quite pleasing when one got over the initial impressions.

Inside, she noted ranks and ranks of WPCs at typewriters, all tapping away. She thought of how her life might have worked out if her papa hadn't been a self-made millionaire in coal. Perhaps she, attracted to the detection business, would have become a WPC herself, tapping away at her desk wearing a smart uniform and receiving several slaps a day on her skirted bottom from male colleagues. She would have been in Swansea, of course, not Inverness, but otherwise it would have been remarkably similar.

Well, that wasn't how it had worked out, so that was that.

Inspector MacB had kindly telephoned ahead to say that the party was arriving and had the various permissions organised. They were swept through the formalities, as if visiting dignitaries, Lady Darriby-Jones expecting to be handed a spade and asked to shovel the first few spades of dirt onto the tree they were planting to commemorate something or other.

Within a few minutes of entering the police station, they were sat in an interview room with a couple of police officers, one quite senior, the other a WPC, no doubt dragged from the typing pool to make up the numbers.

The door opened and the Honourable Frederick Blythe walked in.

In handcuffs. The first thing Lady Darriby-Jones noticed.

"I think they can come off," she said, putting the ice of disapproval into her voice.

Off they came; rank or position in society could be a wonderful thing, she thought.

"Freddie, my dear, how are you?"

"Absolutely fine, aunty, the food here is better than school grub and they've let me do my schoolwork. You know, I've actually finished that essay that was supposed to be done over Christmas. What do you say to that, aunty, not too shabby is it?"

"We're going to get you out of here," Lady Alice said, thinking no doubt back to her own time in jail, just a month earlier. Alfie had manoeuvred it in a brave attempt to safeguard her when Lord Lowell was on the rampage and out for revenge. She had hated the food, particularly the porridge, but clearly Freddie's standards weren't so high.

"I know," he replied. "I know you will because I'm innocent. I would never do what they say I've done."

Lady Darriby-Jones reflected a moment; she was sure there were many procedures that hadn't been followed to the letter with regard to arresting and holding a minor, and the police force was probably embarrassed, the level of embarrassment rising with the individual's seniority. She would press it a little, not too much, because she wanted his freedom as soon as possible and didn't want them battening down the hatches.

She couldn't tell the male officer's rank, so while Alice and Alfie handed over sweets and chocolate to Freddie for consumption back in his cell, she wondered whether this man was senior enough?

"I wanted a private word with you," the male officer said when they eventually stood to go. "You see, I think my boys got a bit carried away with their enthusiasm and forgot some of the rules regarding holding and questioning minors."

Quit when you're ahead, Lady Darriby-Jones thought and smiled graciously at the officer.

. . .

Outside, the short day was at an end. Smith opened the doors for them and prepared to drive away.

"Where now, milady?" he asked, expecting another trip.

"Oh, I think that's enough for one day, Smith. Back to the hotel, if you will. We can regroup and see where we are over supper and a glass of gin. Ah, Alfie, I thought that would make you perk up a bit. My, quite a day it's been."

Smith drove out of the police station and turned right.

"What's that?" Lady Alice cried.

"What's what?"

"The headline on that newspaper stand." They looked and saw:

Headmaster Murdered

"What's it say after that?" Lady Darriby-Jones asked.

"Something to do with being stabbed from behind at his desk," Lady Alice said; with her glasses on, she had perfect eyesight and could see right across the street, even in the pale light of a streetlamp.

"Smith, please stop the car and get a copy. We must know who it is." But Lady Darriby-Jones had a sneaking feeling that she knew exactly who had been murdered.

As if they didn't have enough on their minds already.

Chapter Seven

*I*f you make a plan, you've got to be prepared to break it.

At least that formed a major part of Lady Darriby-Jones' view of the world as she directed Smith to race back to the school. In the back of the Rolls, all three of them poured over the newspaper, relaying snippets of information to Smith, who sped along, eager to cover the twenty-six miles from Inverness to Auchin as quickly as he could.

He knew that when a murder happened, Lady Darriby-Jones liked to be early on the scene. Picking this up from the 'latest, latest, read all about it' brigade at the newsstand meant they would not make it as an early bird.

"There will still be clues. It's just a matter of knowing where to look," Alfie said.

"True," said Lady Darriby-Jones, "but if the local police are anything like the crowd in Darriby, all those clues will be trodden all over by the time we get there."

"Not true, mother," Lady Alice put in, "you see Inspector MacB has an eternity of wisdom and knowledge compared to old Bad Manners. I think you'll find him a cooperative copper, and nothing like as clumsy as Manners."

Nevertheless, Smith picked up on the vibes and pushed the pedal to the floor, making the twenty-six miles fly by. There were a lot of police cars and ambulances scatted around the drive, plus two policemen checking everybody in and out.

"I'm sorry, Lady Darriby-Jones, but I can't let you in. It's a case of officials only, you see."

"We understand," Lady Alice put in before her mother could raise an objection. "Smith, back up and we'll go to the hotel."

"You gave way very easily, Ali," Lady Darriby-Jones said, clearly annoyed at being blocked from entering.

"Gave way, fiddlesticks. Smith, turn here and then next left and the one after. We'll simply go in the back way."

"How do you know about this route?" Lady Darriby-Jones asked as the Rolls bumped along a track that threatened to become no more than a path at any moment.

"Malcolm told me," she replied, making Alfie give her a strange look, which she probably enjoyed. "He explained it as a shortcut to the hotel and I just figured we could use it to get in the back way."

"Good girl, good work."

A few minutes later, they pulled up to what must be the kitchens, evidenced by a pair of rats guarding the entrance to the kitchen yard, before deciding it was all too much bother and skulking away.

Smith came with them this time, sensing danger ahead. They made it through the deserted kitchens, switching the electric oven off where somebody had left it on, but leaving a single line of strip lights in case they needed a quick getaway.

"What are we looking for?" Smith asked.

"Clues," said Lady Alice, not being particularly helpful.

"I see, Lady Alice," he replied, somewhat subdued.

"Anything unusual," Lady Darriby-Jones said, trying to make up for her daughter's rudeness.

They found what you would expect to find in an average run-down boarding school for boys. There were classrooms with rows of desks, complete with copious and occasionally amusing graffiti, changing rooms where the smell of wet clothing became unbearable, store rooms where every food item seemed to be kept in huge industrial containers, and mile upon mile of corridors, with dark green paint to waist level and a lighter shade above.

All standard fare, replicated a thousand times over at boarding schools up and down the country.

They couldn't hope to get into the headmaster's study, the scene of the crime, unless... they were invited.

"Is Inspector MacBride here by any chance?" Alfie asked a police constable who seemed to be on sentry duty but uncertain why he was guarding entry to an empty washroom.

"Yes, sir. Do you want me to fetch him?" The dozy fellow seemed to think Alfie was a senior officer of some description, despite being younger than the constable.

"Yes, tell him Burrows is here. We'll guard this in the meantime." A hint of senior officer status without telling a bare-faced lie.

They checked the washroom, finding plenty of muddy sports kit, but nothing that resembled a clue.

"Ah, Mr Burrows, Lady Darriby-Jones and Lady Alice, what a surprise, but what are you doing in the school at a time like this?"

"Ah, Inspector MacB, how nice to see you," Lady Darriby-Jones replied, thinking anxiously that she needed an angle to get in to the murder scene. "We came to collect some paperwork from Mr Hardway in my capacity as defacto chairwoman of the board of governors." This time the bare-faced lie came from her lips, but she felt it justified. After all, if the chair of the governors had been laid so low to reduce him to grave-level, as everyone seemed to think, Lady Darriby-Jones was the sort they would turn to. There was also the matter of the scholarship fund cheque she had written out and sent back to the bursar just before Christmas.

"Ah, well, I see, that's fine then. In fact, you may be of some use to me as the defacto whatever it was."

"Chairwoman of the board of governors," Lady Alice added. For a moment, she thought her daughter would add a telling off, such as, 'pay attention the first time and there won't be a need for a second explanation'.

But, thankfully, she didn't. Even if she had, Lady Darriby-Jones doubted that Inspector MacB would be seriously put out; it seemed geniality was the core to his particular genetic make-up.

"You see," the inspector continued, "I'm not CID, not a detective at all, just here to support the real police work. Now, they've asked me to sort out a bit of a mess about the succession. Apparently, there were two deputy headmasters..."

"Never a good idea."

"Precisely, as I'm learning at the cost of a splitting headache. Anyway, they're at war over succession plans, both claiming to inherit the throne now that poor Mr Hardway is no longer with us. I thought that, if you were the defacto chairwoman of the board of governors – did I get that right, Lady Darriby-Jones? Good – then you could make a selection and placate the others. Abracadabra, problem solved!"

"Well, I'd be delighted to help, inspector, lead the way."

It was a pitched battle in the headmaster's study with two hot and sweaty middle-aged men close to fisticuffs over the tenure of the headmaster position. Lady Darriby-Jones and her little party, the inspector included, hesitated at the door for a moment, listening to the wild claims going on.

Then she entered and swept all before her. Afterwards, Alfie said she had been regal in her commanding presence. Lady Alice said she had done alright; Lady Darriby-Jones held both bits of praise in equal regard.

You have to take into account who is issuing the praise in the first place.

"And who might you two be?" She fired off a volley before they could challenge her. "One at a time please," she continued, in best schoolmistress tones, "I'll hear from you first."

"I'm Parsons, deputy headmaster and..."

"And I'm Dunnerton, also deputy headmaster. And who might you be?"

This is where the inspector earnt his entire month's salary in a single interjection.

"Do you really mean you don't know Lady Darriby-Jones, chairwoman of the board of governors? Well, I must say, if neither of you are known in the right places, I hardly think your candidature for the top job is a likely prospect."

All eyes now on Lady Darriby-Jones, even Lady Alice was showing interest and support for her performance.

"I do believe," she started, "that the priority right now must be the stability and ongoing routine of the school. I've no doubt that both you gentlemen would be entirely capable of taking on the role, but I'm sure you both agree that we need a less contentious person at the helm right now, lest the rivalries and applaudable ambitions get out of hand."

That got a couple of muttered, "I suppose so," replies from them both, probably mainly happy that the other party wasn't getting the promotion.

It seemed to be working.

Then came the spanner in the works.

"Who will be filling the role on a strictly temporary basis, then?" asked either Parsons or Dunnerton, neither of whom were remarkably similar in many regards.

Heavens! She hadn't thought that far ahead. Who could it be? Then, Lady Alice came to the rescue.

"My mother," she said, doing the regal bit almost as well. "Has decided that the new temporary headmaster, pending the full board decision, should be…"

Was the pause deliberate or not, Lady Darriby-Jones wondered. Afterwards, Lady Alice told her the pause was because her memory had let her down at the last minute and she had to scrabble through her mind to come up with, "Mr Malcolm Robertson."

"Well, I never," was the general response, all wind knocked out of their sails, especially when Lady Darriby-Jones played her ace, dismissing them both with an instruction to run and find Mr Robertson and bid him come to the headmaster's study.

Lady Darriby-Jones had one more task before they had earnt free rein to look through the crime scene at will. Out of the corner of her eye, she had noticed Hardway's much put upon secretary writing a letter at her desk.

"What are you doing?" she asked.

"Oh, eh, I'm writing my letter of resignation. I've had enough of all this. First, Freddie disappears and then…"

"Sorry to interrupt, but you're upset about Freddie?"

"Yes, I was rather fond of the boy. Well, everyone was really. Do you know, Lady Darriby-Jones, what's become of him? Is that why you're here?"

"He's been arrested for the murder of both his parents at his ancestral home on Monday 12th July last year. I don't think he did it and we're trying to prove his innocence. What are you doing?"

"Checking, that's what, just checking the diary for last July. Let me see, it was the last week of term, so a bit odd for a boy to be out and about at home. There were all sorts of things going on, school plays and orchestras, sports day too."

"Have you got any entries for 12th?"

"I'll look, Lady Darriby-Jones. Yes, see, at 11.30am Freddie left for the orthodontist in Inverness. Mr Robertson accompanied him as he had no classes to take that day. See, here's a receipt note for the lunch they had afterwards. Freddie had a banana split for pudding."

"What time did they get back?" Lady Darriby-Jones asked, feeling she was onto something really substantial at long last.

"Oh, they would have had to rush back," she replied. That wasn't good news at all. There was still plenty of daylight left to make his way over to Cosforth House.

"Why?"

"Well, Freddie had a star role in the play that afternoon. He made a wonderful Othello."

"What time?"

"Dress rehearsal at 5pm and the first performance at 8pm."

That put Freddie in the clear; they would have no choice but to release him.

"Thank you, my dear, just one more thing. With Mr Robertson in charge and my overseeing things, can we count on the fact that that letter of resignation won't get signed?"

"What letter?" she replied, tearing the half-drafted letter into little pieces and throwing it in the bin.

Chapter Eight

Inspector MacB was a good friend to have, helpful in all sorts of ways. If they hadn't got into the headmaster's study last night, for instance, they would never have discovered the evidence that proved Freddie's innocence beyond the most unreasonable doubt.

Lady Darriby-Jones spent breakfast the next morning wondering about the other benefits of their excursion into the study complex, several rooms across most of the depth of the school on the west elevation.

They had seen the body, not yet removed. Frankly, Mr Hardway didn't seem anything like as big and imposing when lying immobile on the inner study floor. He had seemed rather like the air had been punched out of him; as his life had gone, ego too, so his size had shrivelled back to normal.

But she had clearly seen the knife wounds in his chest and the neat way (if you can ever call the aggression intended to kill someone as neat) in which the murderer slit his throat, just to be sure.

"Very dead," the inspector had said, to which she had answered something like, "quite so".

She also had time, along with Lady Alice and Alfie, to look into entrances and exits, and this is where it got complicated.

"The suite of rooms consists of six separate rooms," she had started as Smith drove them the night before the short distance to the hotel at close to midnight.

"That's right," Alfie had confirmed, "there's the secretary's office, the main reception room, the inner study, a second study, a storeroom and a bathroom." He got to six by bending back his fingers as he spoke.

"Four of which have direct access on to the main landing."

"There's more to it than that," said Alfie. "They all have external windows that open easily. Only the store room and the secretary's office lack windows, presumably stores and secretaries don't qualify for views and escape routes."

"I can trump that," said Lady Alice, forgetting her rumpus about second-class travel. "Did none of you notice that two of the rooms connect directly to other rooms in the house? One to a bedroom suite at the front of the house and one directly through to the old back stairs, via another little bedroom that one of the teachers must occupy."

Lady Darriby-Jones had noticed, but decided in that instant to let Lady Alice have her moment of glory. She congratulated them both on their observance, but this just created an argument between themselves about who had been the most observant. Lady Darriby-Jones decided to retire from the discussion at that point and, when they arrived back at the hotel, went straight up to bed, professing exhaustion after a long day.

But morning brings fresh ideas and fresh energy, not just physically but also of the mind. What had seemed impossible the night before now became decidedly easy to tackle.

"Problem number one," she said in the deserted snug, other than the four of them, including Smith in their party, "there are too many entrances and exits to make out a clear entrance and exit strategy for our murderer."

She liked terms such as 'entrance and exit strategy'; although she knew it was pompous, rather silly in fact, she still liked to drop phrases like that into her conversation from time to time.

"He or she could have come in one way and out another, milady."

"Excellent point, Smith, first-rate thinking."

"Do you want to know my theory?" Lady Alice suddenly spoke up.

"Go ahead, the floor is yours," that was Alfie, still cross about evidently losing the observance battle the night before.

"I think the murderer was known to the victim because..."

"Because the murderer got behind the victim and stabbed him like that, Lady Alice." Smith stood behind Alfie and grabbed him from the rear, using a coffee spoon as his lethal weapon. Then he sat down, suddenly aware that he had overstepped the mark, if only slightly. "I mean, I'm sorry to jump in and steal yer thunder, Lady Alice."

"That's quite alright," Lady Alice said. "You should have seen his face when you grabbed Mr Burrows from behind like that."

They reached an agreement that (a) the murderer had a variety of entrances and exits, (b) he or she may have been waiting there for his victim or could have arrived after Hardway, (c) it probably was a man because of the force behind the attack, (d) the murderer knew his way around the school and (e) the murderer and the murdered knew each other, such that it wasn't a surprise when the murderer let himself be known to the murdered.

"Oh, another point," Alfie added, "it can't have been an antagonistic meeting because the secretary heard nothing throughout the afternoon and Mr Hardway was quite loud when he wanted to express his disdain for anything."

"It could have been the secretary," Lady Alice added, "she fits every other part of our deduction other than being a man."

But they all agreed that sweet Betty Morrison could not have carried out a nasty premeditated murder.

"Certainly not to then be writing out her resignation letter with all those policemen charging about the place," Lady Darriby-Jones concluded, just as she heard a distant telephone in the other bar. It always made her jump, thinking she would never get used to it, not if she lived to be a hundred.

The call was for her, and it was the inspector.

"Lady Darriby-Jones, good news on the Freddie front," he started as soon as she had confirmed her name rather stiffly down the phone.

"Oh, wonderful. When can we pick him up?"

"As soon as you want. By the way, Chief Super Marsh asked if you could pop in and see him when you're down to pick up Freddie."

"I'd be delighted to." She had guessed correctly that the policeman yesterday was pretty senior. He was also pretty worried about the police treatment of Freddie.

"When do you think that might be, Lady Darriby-Jones?"

"We'll leave immediately. Should be with you in forty minutes."

"Good, I'll tell Mr Marsh to expect you then. No speeding now, at least not on my patch. Goodbye until later, Lady Darriby-Jones."

"Goodbye." She handed the receiver back to Cathy, who seemed always to be around.

"Right, we should be off to pick up Freddie," she said to the others.

"Oh, he's been released then?" Cathy asked, "that is such good news."

Cathy's mixture of surprise and pleasure stayed with Lady Darriby-Jones all the way down to Inverness, still working its way through her mind as she separated herself to see the Chief Super, while the others waited for Freddie to be released.

The Chief Super couldn't have been nicer. Lady Darriby-Jones almost asked whether it was obligatory north of the border to be nice when in a blue uniform. But she didn't, preferring to let him concentrate on what he wanted to get off his chest.

Which was quite a lot.

"First of all, nobody should have boarded a train to arrest a sixteen-year-old on his way back to school."

"I agree, Mr Marsh."

"And he should not have been questioned about anything without a guardian or other adult present. You may recall me saying that I'd been called in to investigate the handling of this and there's some pretty extensive training about to start, the aim being to re-educate certain officers as to proper procedure."

"That seems a sensible course of action."

"I just," suddenly Mr Marsh seemed much less certain about things, "I just wanted to…"

"Did you meet Freddie, Mr Marsh?"

"No, I didn't have that pleasure, at least not until yesterday when I accompanied your visit with him."

"If you had had the opportunity to get to know him, and I understand your time is limited, you would realise that whatever your concerns might be, Freddie is not the type to take any advantage or try and extract some benefit from the situation. He's just not like that."

"Well, frankly, that's a huge relief. Thank you, Lady Darriby-Jones, for your understanding."

"Think nothing of it, Mr Marsh. Your people have been kind and helpful when several Sassenachs turned up on your patch a few days ago. Inspector MacBride has been a complete gentleman and we haven't met a cross copper anywhere."

"Even the one who turned you away at the school gates yesterday evening?"

"You know about him? Not that he was unfair or impolite, just firm about his duty."

"MacB and I go back a long way, Lady Darriby-Jones. I was his first sergeant about a hundred years ago. I also took the liberty of telephoning the Chief Constable of Oxfordshire Constabulary."

"Ah, Bertie."

"Bertie to you, very much 'sir' to me! But his deputy told me some astounding things about you and your detecting work. Lord Lowell, for instance, quite a catch!"

"I had a lot of people helping me."

"All I wanted to say, Lady Darriby-Jones, before I let you go to see your nephew, is that we really enjoy you staying up here and if you should so happen to decide to stay a while longer, there's quite a mystery surrounding the Blythes of Cosforth that I really think you could turn your mind to."

"That's very kind of you, Mr Marsh. I'll have to consult with Freddie, of course. I had rather thought to take him back to Darriby for a rest after his rather strenuous ordeal."

"I quite understand, Lady Darriby-Jones, but the offer is there if you want it."

Freddie was consulted. Lady Darriby-Jones knew what his response would be but decided to have a bit of fun about it when she got to see him on his release a few minutes later. After the initial hugs and expressions of joy, Lady Darriby-Jones seemed to take control.

"Right," she said, "into the car with you all. We've got a long drive ahead. You two jailbirds," she continued, pointing at Lady Alice and Freddie, "can regale us with stories of the chain gang while we travel south." She winked quickly at Smith, who caught on and went to open the car doors.

"Come along, young sirs and Lady Alice. We've got a long way to go if we are to do half the journey by nightfall."

"Are we going back to Darriby, then?" Freddie asked, "I mean, what about all the things going on here?"

"What things?"

"Well, there's school for a start. My exams aren't over yet."

"You've never cared about exams before. See here, Freddie, it's a straight choice between going to back to Darriby for some nice quiet days by the fire and going for long walks across the estate, or we stay here and have to spend time solving the mystery of who killed Mr Hardway."

The others had guessed, now, all made small talk about how beautiful Darriby was in the dead of winter, also about loving some peace and quiet.

"Are we a democracy?" Freddie asked.

"We are," Lady Alice replied, "but you're too young to vote." This was dangerous grounds for Lady Alice because she, as a woman, did not have the vote, although she vaguely supported the suffragette movement when it didn't clash with her riding.

"I'm taller than you," was Freddie's reply.

"Alright, let's put it to a vote then. All in favour of going quietly home to Darriby, raise your hands."

Nobody did.

"You rotters. You never did intend going back to Darriby."

"Maybe we didn't," said Lady Darriby-Jones, while scribbling a quick note to Chief Superintendent Marsh. "Maybe we didn't."

Chapter Nine

The breakfast table was crowded now, with five of them around a table designed for four and heaped with bacon, eggs, sausages, mushrooms and toast and marmalade. Smith had offered to sit at a separate table, but Lady Darriby-Jones would hear nothing of it.

"This is our main briefing time, Smith, and, like it or not, you're part of the team now."

"Yes, milady," a standard response, but it hid a great deal of pride he felt at his inclusion.

"First stop," said Lady Darriby-Jones, between nibbles of toast, "is back to school for Freddie."

"But it's exam time, I thought..."

"You've changed your tune suddenly," Lady Alice said, making Lady Darriby-Jones think hard about her daughter; she really was in quite a crosspatch mood, more so than usual, although she was often snappy and lacking in patience.

"I want to be involved with the investigations," Freddie replied, "not stuck doing a miserable Latin exam."

"That's precisely my point, Freddie. You see, we need an inside man. With the death of Mr Hardway, the school becomes a pretty important focal point for our investigations. We need someone on the inside who can feed us all the information about what's going on."

"I see, but can't you get me off Latin? I hate it so."

"That would be too suspicious, young Mr Freddie," Smith spoke up suddenly, "I mean, someone with an exemption from exams would make me suspicious, especially if I had something to hide. We want you to be someone who people reveal things to, not someone the baddies steer clear of."

"Well said, Smith, I couldn't have put it better myself," said Lady Alice, getting a tongue poked out very close to her in response, "Eek, you're disgusting, Freddie, now I'm going to have to have a bath and change my clothes."

"Go on then, Cousin Ali." But she didn't move, not wanting to lose out on their briefing session.

Which wrapped up pretty soon afterwards because Lady Darriby-Jones didn't have any idea of what to brief her team on, other than to go forth and investigate, which sounded a little corny so she bypassed that closing comment and stood from the breakfast table.

"Right, all squared away with breakfast? Let's be off in ten minutes, then."

. . .

There was a group of journalists at the front gate to the school. Smith slowed down on Lady Darriby-Jones' instruction and they spent ten minutes, not a moment longer, asking questions from the press.

Ten minutes proved long enough, for Freddie and Lady Alice both started to get silly, exaggerating Freddie's time in the dungeons, with Lady Alice adding that she had been kidnapped and falsely imprisoned just back before Christmas.

"So, you know what it's like then, my dear?"

"My name is Lady Alice."

"So, you know what it's like then, Lady Alice, my dear?"

"Time to go, ladies and gents. We've got a lot to do today." They parted to let the car through, but kept asking questions.

Lady Darriby-Jones had telephoned the school from the hotel to say they would be in shortly. Old Ma Bosom was waiting patiently for them at the bottom of the gate. As they drove up the drive, they could see her doing giant sideway steps with her uniform dress tucked between her legs like a huge wrestler dominating the ring.

"Oh, I didn't see you there," she said, quickly smoothing her dress and checking her hair beneath her cap. "It's quite blowy today, isn't it? Right then, Blythe, let's get you checked out and on into class. You've missed the first two periods, but you should catch..."

"Latin," shouted Lady Alice from the car.

"How on earth did you know?" matron asked.

"Oh, I just knew. I carry a lot of knowledge around inside me."

Old Ma Bosom smiled as she led Freddie away by the hand. Lady Darriby-Jones watched from the back of the car, thinking her nephew, of sorts, was suddenly rather vulnerable as he walked up the steps.

"He'll need some new uniforms," Old Ma called back from the top step.

"Put it on the account," Lady Darriby-Jones replied.

"I'll see what I can find. Where on earth has he been?" Then they were inside and Lady Darriby-Jones felt very much like she did when they had tried Lady Alice at boarding school, as if she had left half of her behind in the school.

Two further events happened that day. First, Inspector MacB came to the hotel looking for them.

"I hear from the Chief Super that you're on the case," he said as soon as he saw Lady Darriby-Jones.

"I said we'd try and help while we're here, but we don't want to get in your way."

"Far from it. I'm looking forward to all the help I can get. It's not often that you get a murder like this one in your backyard."

"Nor the mystery of the murder that may not even be a murder," she replied, after ordering a large pot of coffee.

"You think they're still alive?"

"I don't know, really I don't. I just have a feeling that somebody would have found some evidence of something by now."

"Well," said the inspector, "on the school murder, we're working on two parallel lines, maybe more like divergent lines than parallel. We're going on the possibility that this was a crime of opportunity on the one hand and a crime of intense passion on the other."

"My vote is the latter, for what it's worth."

"I tend to agree, Lady Darriby-Jones." That set her reflecting that if she had tried to hold such a frank discussion with Rory 'Bad' Manners, the DCI back home, she would have been met with ridicule and sarcasm mounting up on each other.

It was nice to be away for a while, just as it would be nice to go back home again. Had she done the right thing in getting Freddie to stay? She could fool herself that it had been Freddie's choice, but she had led the discussion in such a way that he was bound to say 'yes'.

The second event that day happened much later during supper. Cathy seemed to dedicate herself to their table that night, always being there and taking great care with serving the food and refilling wine glasses.

"You're very attentive, Cathy," she observed when Smith had retired for the night and the other two had gone to play darts in the pub. Another spat had occurred when Alfie had said they may not approve of dart-hurling ladies and she had replied that she would do as she liked and she didn't care two figs, not even one fig, whether people approved of her actions or not.

At least they were playing together, something they wouldn't have done when they got off the train at Inverness a few days ago.

"I wanted a word, Miss, I mean milady."

"Well, take the weight off your feet and tell me all about it."

"It's just that I know something about Freddie, I mean."

For the briefest of moments, Lady Darriby-Jones thought she was going to dish the dirt on Freddie, come up with some terrible proof that he was, after all, involved in the murder of both parents. She saw herself as his last friend, walking with him to the gallows, trying to comfort someone who would not be comforted.

For the simple reason that Freddie was in love with life and would never want to let it go, not without a long innings at the crease first.

Then, after looking at Cathy a moment, it came to her, making sense at long last.

"It's about the letters, isn't it? The ones that were sent to the newspaper."

"It is, yes."

"It's because you sent them?"

"I did, I thought it would be…"

"Fun?"

"Yes fun, I mean Freddie and I wrote them together, but I was the leader, the one who suggested it. I even thought it might be a basis for a comic book story, like the ones you can get in the shop."

"You should really have destroyed them after writing them. The actual writing is one thing, but sending them to the newspaper is another thing altogether."

"Plus, I was too scared to do anything about it. I should have owned up to stop Freddie being charged."

"He wasn't charged. He was released without anything so much as a warning."

She stopped talking for a moment, idly polishing the table top, pouring on far too much polish and then smearing it until it eventually sought another residence, by way of dripping onto the floor.

"There's another thing," she said, and this time Lady Darriby-Jones had no idea what would come next.

"What's that?" If in doubt, ask.

"I don't believe Freddie's parents are dead."

"Why's that?" But she didn't get a proper answer, not one the police would believe to be sufficient to reopen a case once closed, in the sense that they assumed the parents to be deceased. Instead, she gave a long story about how the earl and countess had come to stay at their hotel once. "And she sat in the very chair that you're now sitting in."

"Cathy, Cathy, where are you?" The voice came fluttering across the pub and into the restaurant at the back. "We're one person down and we've got a pile of dirty dishes to do."

"Coming, coming, coming," she replied, jumping to her feet and brushing her apron and skirt into place.

"Let's talk more tomorrow," she whispered as she gave the tiniest of curtseys. "I do know something that will interest you."

"What is..." But she was gone, fading into the pub as if she were a ghost from long ago.

Chapter Ten

It had to be the most frustrating of days. It started full of hope and togetherness as they made their way, after breakfast, to Auchin School for Boys.

"Hello, Betty, we're here to see Freddie, of course, but I'd also like a word with Mr Robertson if that's possible."

"Oh, well..."

"Is something the matter, Betty?"

"Something most definitely is the matter," came a strange voice from the top of the main staircase, once something pretty grand but worn by several generations of boys who had, inadvertently or on purpose, knocked off the various ornate parts, just as they had scuffed the wood varnish with their rugger boots in winter and cricket boots in summer. In all likelihood, several headmasters will have tried to put the main stairs out of bounds, sending the kids to one of several staircases at the back of the house. Except, the natural law of boyhood dictates that you can't send a boy the long way around, especially if there are no bannisters to slide down.

But this was no boy preparing to slide down the bannisters to land in a pile at their feet. This was an imposing man in his fifties, who looked remarkably like Freddie, except shorter, plumper, more cross and more red-faced as a result. But otherwise, it was Freddie.

If Lady Darriby-Jones hadn't known the Earl of Cosforth, she would have sworn they had found Freddie's papa.

"My name is Lady Darriby-Jones," she said, as clearly as she could muster with the level of confusion she felt; then, quite suddenly, it all fitted together. "You must be Major Blythe, Freddie's uncle."

"Darriby-Jones, eh? Not the blighter who married the coalminer's daughter." Well, thought Lady Darriby-Jones, he's got that the wrong way around and is being pretty rude into the bargain. "You're the blighter's guardian, aren't you?"

She was about to point out that she was modelled on Eve rather than Adam, going one short on the rib front, plus lacking entirely the bobbly bit in the throat she never could remember the name of. But he beat her to it with a further accusation.

"So, you must be the blighter who appointed Robertson as headmaster yesterday. I mean Robertson, can you ever believe it?" His chortle, which he exhibited with powerful lungs and a surprisingly beautiful voice, didn't match Freddie's laugh at all; next point of divergence, there actually being quite a few when she considered it.

The Mystery of the Murder that Wasn't

Freddie would never categorise everybody as blighters and he would never dream of being rude; it just wasn't in him.

"I did, in my capacity as acting chair of the board of governors. I believe one is perfectly entitled to make such appointments in the name of the board.

"Well, Jones, or whatever your real name is, I've got some news for you. This is my school, so I can do what I like with it. I'm back as headmaster and I'm dealing with the mess that everyone has created in recent months during my absence. It's my school and I've reappointed myself as headmaster."

"Really?" She was on uncertain ground here. Some schools, she knew, were owned by the 'blighters' who ran them, but most were put in trust, which meant a board of governors. Plus, this was the man who had recently retired. "I thought you had retired from the profession, Major Blythe?"

"What?" he seemed likely to explode; certainly, his body temperature was rising, evidenced in the redness to his face. To Lady Darriby-Jones, no medical whiz kid, he looked like heart attack material. She expected him to clutch his left breast at any moment and keel over, tumbling down the stairs to the landing.

The question had to be asked; why such anger?

"I want you out of here now." He was raising the stakes and Lady Darriby-Jones didn't know how to respond.

So Alfie stepped in. Or rather he stepped up, several steps with each bound until he was at the first floor, level with Major Blythe.

"Perhaps we can talk about this, Major Blythe?" he said calmly.

"Who the blazes is this blighter?" the major replied, reaching new levels of rudeness by not even addressing him, displaying a rather amateurish and cruel classroom technique by speaking to the entire class and putting the subject down as a third party.

"I am Alfred Burrows, personal secretary to the Darriby-Jones family," he said, forcing a smile onto his face. "We're helping with some enquiries..."

"You're not police, are you?"

"No, but we're..."

"Then get out. Miss Morrison, see these blighters out of my school at once."

"Yes, Major Blythe, at once." *The poor girl deserves better,* Lady Darriby-Jones thought. *Two headmasters in a row, both pure bullies and nasty pieces of work. A brief respite with the gentle Mr Robertson, no more than a day it would seem, and now back to the original firebrand of a man.* "If you would be kind enough to come this way."

Lady Darriby-Jones thought it, on balance, wise to move away from this odious man, but Alfie and Lady Alice thought differently, especially when the major gave Alfie a shove on the top step, making Alfie tumble down the stairs to the large landing.

Lady Alice was up the steps even more quickly than Alfie had managed it. She was also more cunning, putting her back to the bannisters so it wouldn't be so easy to dislodge her.

The Mystery of the Murder that Wasn't

"If you've hurt Mr Burrows, you'll have me to answer to. That's a fact." From a floor below, she looked convincing enough, pummelling a fist into an open palm, glaring defiance from every pore of her body, but the major simply turned and walked away, shouting something about Miss Morrison getting rid of the scum contaminating his school.

Surprisingly, it was Betty Morrison who thought to attend to Alfie, much to Lady Darriby-Jones' shame. She went quietly up the steps and knelt at the body, probing limbs after checking for a pulse.

"I think it's a sprain," she called down below. "We have a nurse in the village. No broken bones, thank goodness."

Outside, on the drive, Betty Morrison apologised for the aggression of her old boss, who had, it appears, suddenly become her new boss.

"What happened to Mr Robertson?" Lady Darriby-Jones asked.

"I'm afraid he was no match for Major Blythe, Lady Darriby-Jones. He was dismissed immediately Major Blythe returned and told to leave the premises, much like..."

"Much like us, yes, I can understand how it must have been. And Freddie?"

"Oh, he seems to have bounced back, Lady Darriby-Jones. Although he claims exemption from all exams this term, says the police psychologist, whatever that is, said it might be too much stress for him, given what he's been through."

"I can't imagine Major Blythe taking that well."

"Oh, he didn't. He just told him to get down to the main hall and get on with his Latin exam! Gave him an almighty kick on his backside, 'to help him on his way'."

"I can just picture that," Lady Alice said, then returned to her self-appointed role of guiding Alfie towards the car as if he had broken his leg in several places rather than sprained a wrist.

They regrouped back at the hotel around a pot of steaming hot coffee, just the way Lady Darriby-Jones liked it.

"The big thing I don't understand," she said, "is why Major Blythe bothered to come back to the school at all."

"Oh, I know the answer to that." They all looked up to see Cathy MacIntyre standing, her hands folded over her white apron, just as a domestic should. But her green eyes blazed fires of their own and Lady Darriby-Jones knew she had some involvement in the strange events at the school. Also, she remembered there was a confession she was going to make the night before; the conversation had gone clean out of Lady Darriby-Jones' mind.

But confessions were less likely to be fulsome when the confessor was obliged to perform in front of a crowd.

"Smith, please be so kind as to take Mr Burrows and Lady Alice down to the police station. The three of you could liaise with the inspector and report back to me on any new findings." They knew they were being dismissed for a purpose. All rose immediately as Smith said the car would be brought around to the front of the hotel in a few minutes' time.

"Take a seat, Miss MacIntyre, it's time we had a chat. Grab a cup and saucer if you want any of this delicious coffee you made for us." Most people would reject the offer of coffee, given that she was a maid about to sit and confess to a lady, but Cathy went without a word to the sideboard and collected the cup and saucer, before sitting down in the chair Smith had occupied a moment ago.

"Where do we start?" Lady Darriby-Jones said when Cathy had poured herself a cup and refilled Lady Darriby-Jones' one.

"First, I'm not a witch."

"I never thought you were, my dear." That wasn't quite true; she remembered the upsetting dream a few nights ago, featuring a witch's hat.

"Everybody thinks I am. It's the green eyes and black hair."

"Well, to be honest, you also seem to have a fascination with... what's it called now?"

"The macabre, Lady Darriby-Jones."

"Yes, the macabre MacIntyre." Cathy took a moment to process the little joke, then her face broke out into a broad smile and Lady Darriby-Jones knew that she was only guilty of what Freddie was guilty of.

That being an exuberance that knew no bounds.

"The confession, Cathy? What you were going to say last night?"

"Oh, yes. Well, I sent those letters to the newspaper and got my Freddie into such a mess because of my foolishness."

"You did, my dear." Lady Darriby-Jones was always a sucker for the straightforward types, liking the direct speaking and relishing the lack of subtleness that others seemed to want to employ. It was one, amongst many, of the reasons why she had taken to Freddie so well.

But Cathy had said 'my Freddie', which meant there was a romantic element to all this. She would have to tread carefully.

"Why did you say that about Major Blythe?" she asked, skipping the rest of the romantic entanglement bit, thinking it was too complicated for now.

"Because he never wanted to retire as headmaster. I typed the copies for the board of governors' meeting last summer and they discussed how he was becoming quite impossible. The earl wanted to give him another chance, but he was outvoted."

"Interesting." In more ways than one; it meant there was a board of governors, so her appointment of Mr Robertson wasn't valid at all. But where were they? Well, two, the earl and the countess, had been despatched to the great school in the sky, but if the earl was outvoted, that implied there was at least a third member.

"Also," Cathy added, meaning a trio of revelations. "There's something fishy going on in the school."

"What do you mean?"

"I work in the accounts department, just as a clerk and part time. That's how I got to meet my Freddie in the first place."

"And?"

"Well, there's some strange receipts going through for..."

Lady Darriby-Jones never heard what the receipts consisted of, for the door burst open and her three fellow investigators came charging in.

"You've got to come quickly," three voices mingled. "They've only gone and arrested Mr Robertson for the murder of Hardway."

Chapter Eleven

Lady Darriby-Jones had that feeling that everything was moving too fast, with interruptions to the interruptions and nothing quite reaching a conclusion. She would have liked to concentrate on one piece of the puzzle at a time, but had so many considerations to take on board.

Had the earl and countess been murdered?

If so, who had done it?

If no murder, there was a big mystery surrounding the murder that wasn't, specifically, what had become of Freddie's parents?

Moving on, there was a murder without doubt. Hardway lay on a cold slab in the morgue in Inverness. Who had decided to do away with him?

Presumably, not Malcolm Robertson, who, Ali had told her, was nicknamed St Malcolm for his kind and gentle ways, seeming so incongruous with the rough nature of the school.

And then, what role did young Cathy MacIntyre play in this? She felt sure it was closer to mischievousness than evil, but there definitely was something to investigate.

Finally, who was the mysterious third board member who had, presumably, voted against the continuation of Major Blythe as headmaster of Auchin School for Boys?

So many questions and puzzles that she really did not know where to start.

Well, when nothing fitted together, Lady Darriby-Jones knew, from long experience, that the best thing to do was nothing.

By which she meant, let events come to her rather than seeking them out.

"Tell all," she said to her colleagues as Cathy slipped away, mumbling something about fresh coffee, and they took their old places back again.

"We went to the local police station and met with Inspector MacB, just as you told us to," Alfie said.

"He's only gone and arrested St Malcolm." Lady Alice was the type who latched on to nicknames in a flash, putting quite a lot of energy into developing them as well. Lady Darriby-Jones wouldn't be surprised if she had a new variant for Mr Robertson before the story was fully out. "You couldn't get a more decent fellow than the sainted prof."

"What's the basis for the arrest?" Lady Darriby-Jones asked, noting the progression of nicknames she had predicted.

Alfie took over then, it feeling like more of a secretarial function to report on actual events in a dispassionate manner, rather than permit the extraordinary mixture of instinct and emotion that Lady Alice brought to the table.

He explained that the only other person on the first floor at that time, roughly a quarter past six in the evening, had been Mr Robertson, who had a tiny bedroom and study combined at the back of the house on the western side.

"There's a door that links his study-bedroom to the suite that Mr Hardway used for his offices. The door goes to the bathroom, which Mr Robertson was in the habit of using as the only other bathroom on that floor is at the other end of the house. From the bathroom, you nip across the larger study and straight from there into the private study where the murder took place."

"The police have established that no one else was on the first floor?"

"Betty goes home at six. She actually left five minutes early that day for a doctor's appointment and met Cathy in the entrance hall. They walked together to the village. The murder couldn't have happened before that because of Hardway's wristwatch."

"What significance does the wristwatch have?" This was new to Lady Darriby-Jones. She knew there was a growing fashion for wristwatches, but failed to see how they could pinpoint the time of death.

"It was smashed in the attack and the exact time was 6.15. Therefore, it's a fairly safe guess that the murder happened around that time. Of course, the murderer could have played with the watch arms to alter the time, but I tend to agree with the police that this was a crime with a high degree of passion involved and not committed by someone into precise planning and scheming to hide his or her tracks."

"Good point," Lady Darriby-Jones conceded, then started wondering who could be passionate enough to do such a thing?

Cathy brought fresh coffee and Lady Darriby-Jones decided, on impulse, to include her in the discussions.

"Cathy, my dear, pull up a chair if you have a moment to spare. We want to ask you some questions. But first, I want to know about Freddie's daily routine and when it is that you can see him."

"Certainly, Lady Darriby-Jones." Could her willingness to participate be from a feeling of guilt? Or was she just a decent young girl who had taken a shine for Freddie?

She detailed the school timetable, not so much the lessons which varied by class, but when meals were, when they went to chapel or had free time, and when they had showers and trooped off to bed.

"Freddie's in Upper Five," she said, "that means in the dorms by 9 o'clock and lights out thirty minutes later. I finish at six on the days I'm in and often hang around to see Freddie when he has a break after study period which ends at seven-thirty. I used to sneak into the kitchens and pinch some chocolate biscuits they give out to the boys after

The Mystery of the Murder that Wasn't

study time. We would share them around the back of the school, even though that's out of bounds by the dustbins, both for Freddie and for me. I risked getting fired and Freddie faced the cane if caught, but we loved that feeling of breaking the rules."

"So, you could get a message to Freddie this evening? Because we want to get Alfie and Lady Alice into the school tonight, while Smith and I wait in the car. Can you set up a meeting between them? That way, we can get a full update from Freddie as to what's going on."

"Yes, I can do that," Cathy replied, no doubt loving the intrigue and adventure involved.

"Excellent. Now, one more thing," Lady Darriby-Jones said, "you were telling me before about some strange receipts passing through the accounts office. Can you tell us more about what you're seeing?"

"Well, it might be nothing at all, milady, but it's just that there are some receipts for groceries to be delivered every week to some place. The bill doesn't give a delivery address and that's what is odd. Normally, the bills will give the school address and mark down something about the delivery. These ones just say, 'sundry groceries as ordered and delivered' and then the price."

"Can you smuggle some out to show us?"

"Oh, yes, that would be fun. I'm sure I could do that. Now, I'm going to be late for my other job at the school so I'd better be going. I'll let you know about contact with Freddie later today when I get back but it seems to be full steam ahead for adventure!"

. . .

Lady Darriby-Jones suggested no headlights as the Rolls crept up the back track they had used before to get into the house. They parked behind the stables and she wished Lady Alice and Alfie good luck with their venture.

"Remember," she said, "this is to get contact with Freddie and to get a report as to what he's found out. It's only necessary because Major Blythe won't let us near the place. The sooner we get Major Blythe away from the school and not the headmaster any longer, the better."

"But he's been officially appointed," Alfie pointed out.

"Yes, but by whom?" If only she knew she would be able to apply some pressure. "Got your torches? Good, don't use them unless you have to. Freddie should be in the changing rooms on the ground floor. You've memorised the plan of the house Cathy did for you? Excellent, we hope to see you inside the hour. Good luck, now."

It's almost as hard to wait as it is to act a part in a true adventure, defined as one where there was real risk. The wait is agonising, particularly as time slows right down when all one can do is twiddle one's thumbs and wonder what the active bods are going through.

It was just so for Smith and Lady Darriby-Jones. The night was all around them, actually no light anywhere until you got to the school where there were a couple of night lights left on. Presumably they were to facilitate bathroom visits in the middle of the night without risk of broken limbs or losing one's way and ending up back in the wrong dorm.

The Mystery of the Murder that Wasn't

There were sounds, of course, but no human sounds, just foxes and owls and other nocturnal beasts going about their business. Smith, in the front, didn't talk to Darriby-Jones in the back, and Darriby-Jones chose not to break her silence either. The only other noise was the clicking of the engine as it cooled and that grew steadily less and less frequent.

Lady Darriby-Jones had no way to tell the time. She considered asking Smith, but, strangely, didn't want to break the silence. She tried counting, but counting sent her to sleep and she didn't want to miss any of the action.

What action? Everything was peaceful and quiet, just another night in the Highland winter, cold, dark and frosty.

It was definitely a shotgun, both bores in rapid succession. Lady Darriby-Jones knew enough about guns to recognise the blast from a 12-bore.

"Start the engine," she blurted to Smith, who woke suddenly from his slumber and did as he was told. Then she noticed lights blaring from the back of the house, flicking on in room after room, presumably someone searching through the ground floor, seeking intruders.

"Be ready to go," she told Smith, who confirmed his readiness. "No lights yet." It was important not to give away their position before they had to. There would be some explaining to do to Darriby if the Rolls was peppered with shot.

"Someone's coming, milady." Smith had his window wound down to help him detect sound. Now, she could hear it too, someone running towards them at top speed. Lady Darriby-Jones leant forward and opened the door just as a figure crashed through it and landed in a ball on the floor of the car.

"Drive, drive," said Lady Alice. "They've got Alfie already."

Smith needed no more encouragement. Having noted the layout on the way in, he could guide the car out again without the lights, not using them until they were safely away on the main road again.

"What happened?"

"Alfie took a shot, running away, waiting..." Lady Alice couldn't get out any more words than the basics; they would have to wait for an explanation.

Chapter Twelve

Could it get any worse? Lady Darriby-Jones' hastily adopted protégé, St Malcolm, son of Robert, arrested for murder and Alfie Burrows, private secretary and a third of their collective brain power, held in police custody, she imagined for trespass or, more likely if the police were involved, breaking and entering.

She had called Inspector MacB first thing in the morning, wanting to explain what had gone on and seeking Alfie's release. She had been met with politeness that went without saying, but also with a firmness and reserve that caught her by surprise.

It would seem that the inspector was having second thoughts about the involvement of the amateur band of detectives from distant Oxfordshire. Perhaps Major Blythe had an in with the chief super or some other high-ranking police officer.

Lady Alice had been able to confirm that Major Blythe had been behind the shooting. Not from sight, because other than the flash as the barrels went off, there had been total darkness in the school.

"I heard him shout, 'take that you little so-and-so', just before the shots blasted through the room. Mr Burrows, dear Alfie, was down on the ground by my side and whispered to me to get out and that he'd taken a shot in his rear end but would survive. He was so brave, mother, I..." She ran out of words to describe what she felt that moment. No doubt she would soon revert to her usual arrogant state, but those shotgun pellets had done more than blasted through Alfie's bottom, that was for sure.

Lady Darriby-Jones had a wicked thought at that moment that her daughter and Alfie might become an item. He was decidedly lower or middle class and without money, but he had intelligence and courage. Besides, Lady Alice would have plenty of money when Lady Darriby-Jones went off to the great detective convention in the sky, maybe in fifty or sixty years-time.

A wicked thought, not because it was outrageous, but because it was inappropriate at that moment. She had two innocents wrongly incarcerated and depending on her for salvation; she needed to concentrate.

Especially as the situation had just got a lot worse.

Some enterprising copper had realised that St Malcolm had studied at Oxford. Alfie Burrows, just a few years younger than the sainted person, had grown up in Oxford before she had snatched him away to Darriby

It wasn't much work to establish a few connections between them. They tried churches and public houses, before realising that Alfie only occasionally went to church and St Malc was a Methodist, hence strictly off the drink.

Then they stumbled on an obscure playhouse they had both acted at, although not for long in either case as they had both come to terms with the fact that they weren't likely to find fame and fortune on the stage. But, now the police had a connection and endless questions would be put to them to build on this tenuous start.

"It doesn't make any sense that they were working together against Hardway," Lady Alice said. "Granted, our patron saint doesn't have an alibi for the murder time, being in the building and on the same floor as Hardway, but Alfie was actually in Inverness police station when it all happened."

"Neither of them had anything to do with it," Lady Darriby-Jones replied. "Neither are capable of murder and that's a fact."

"Yes, mother, but it's for us to prove that. The police only have to suspect something and now they've got the connection. They think Alfie and St Malc were friends in Oxford and now they're in cahoots up here."

"It really couldn't get any worse," she replied, aware that she needed to buck up and get to grips with the problem, although sometimes she found that you have to force yourself down to rock bottom first, then the only way to go is up.

. . .

A moment later, another maid brought the news that the police were on the line and would Lady Darriby-Jones be so kind as to follow her to the telephone?

"I wonder who that could be," she said.

"Probably your chief super friend from Inverness."

And that's exactly who it was.

"Marsh here," came the voice she had last heard strained with the embarrassment of the mistreatment of Freddie by the police.

"Hello, Mr Marsh, what can I do for you?" Although she knew how this conversation was likely to develop.

"It seems, Lady Darriby-Jones, that we have an unusual development on our hands concerning your private secretary and a certain young teacher. The teacher, a Mr…" there was a pause while he obviously looked through his notes, "yes, Mr Robertson has been charged with murder and is being transferred at this moment to prison on remand. Mr Burrows, on the other hand, is being held on a charge of trespass."

"Not breaking and entering?"

"No, it transpires that the kitchen door was opened from the inside and not forced from the outside. That means the charge can never be more than trespass, which will be a relief to you, I'm sure. However, it does raise the distinct possibility of further collusion in this unhappy series of incidences starting with the murder of Mr Hardway on…"

"Let me stop you there, Mr Marsh."

"Go ahead, Lady Darriby-Jones. The pulpit is yours." For the tenth or twelfth time, Lady Darriby-Jones picked up pleasurably on the enormous politeness every copper north of the border seemed to possess. If that could be magicked up in Oxfordshire, the Darriby world would be improved out of all recognition.

"I believe the series of incidences goes right back to the disappearance of the earl and countess last summer."

"Disappearance?"

"Yes, I no longer believe they were murdered." She hoped the chief super would take this at face value and move on; she was acting on the hunch of all hunches and had little better than zero capability to prove it.

"An interesting theory," he seemed to be moving on. Life just got brighter.

"It puts a different perspective on things, don't you think?"

They batted this way and that for a few more minutes before Mr Marsh announced that (a) he had a pretty good idea, in deed a virtual certainty, of who had been the inside man for last night, adding that boy might be more appropriate than man in this case. And the (b) of it all was that Mr Burrows would be freed.

"It seems we've got some grounds for suspecting that these two knew each other in Oxford, but if you give me your word, Lady Darriby-Jones, as to his innocence, I'll accept that. I also believe he might do more good on the outside as your assistant than rotting on remand awaiting a trial that may never happen."

"Gladly, Mr Marsh, you have my word."

"Excellent, and you'll keep Mr Burrows and your daughter away from any more break-in scenarios?"

"I will, without a doubt." This was an easy promise to make because her plans, finally emerging, were moving in a different direction altogether.

"Finally, a word of advice from an old hand, if you would like it, that is."

"Please advise away, Mr Marsh, I'm never one to ignore the wisdom from experience."

"I learnt over my years in the force that if you have a hunch to back it. No, not just back it but concentrate on it. If you believe that Cosforth and his wife are still of this world, I strongly urge you to back that to the hilt."

"Meaning?" She knew what he meant, but it was as well to get things certain, in black and white, beyond misunderstanding.

"Find them, Lady Darriby-Jones, find them."

Lady Darriby-Jones placed the receiver back on its cradle, the same with the mouthpiece, and went in search of Smith and Lady Alice.

For the first time since the long journey up to Scotland, she felt she had a plan.

Or at least a direction in which her planning could lead.

Chapter Thirteen

If you want a job done well, do it yourself; that's a maxim that Lady Darriby-Jones held sacred, and proved the value of time and time again. She knew that it didn't fit well with the principle of delegation, but swore by it anyway. Alfie and Lady Alice had tried and failed to get into Auchin School for Boys, defeated by the vigilance and determination of Major Blythe.

Where they had failed, she would have a go and felt reasonably confident of success, especially after quizzing Cathy a little more and including the young girl in her fledgling plans. Yes, they had been advised by the chief super to concentrate on the disappearance of the Blythes, implying that he would prefer the Darriby team to stay away from Auchin School, but she would only do that after one more attempt to meet up with Freddie. Hence, she instructed Cathy to put the word out to her nephew that she herself would make the attempt the very next night.

She and Cathy had put together a plan that had to work.

"Make sure Freddie knows that I won't attempt to get in the same way that Alfie and Lady Alice tried. Just tell him to expect a different approach and stay alert," she said to Cathy as she concluded the briefing.

"I understand, milady and will pass the message on." Cathy's facial expression gave away that she considered Lady Darriby-Jones rather an odd lady, but certainly one it was fun to be around. At suppertime in the hotel (there being nowhere else to eat in Auchin other than the chippie which they'd already done with the family MacB), Cathy confirmed that the message had been passed on and Freddie was delighted and excited to receive the news.

"What do you want us to do," Alfie asked, seeming a bit at a loose end. If Alfie was at a loose end, Lady Alice certainly would be, although she seemed back in her morose cocoon, not really willing to engage with the world around her. Lady Darriby-Jones ached to discover what ailed her usually forthright daughter, but had to conclude that it would be best to put her concerns in this regard on the back burner and worry about them later.

At the moment, they had the mystery of all mysteries to solve and it was going to take every scrap of energy and brain power they could muster.

They didn't even know how many murders had been committed. Lady Darriby-Jones felt the world on her shoulders, with tasks stretching out to kingdom come.

And starting with her endeavours that night, for which she required suitable clothing.

The Mystery of the Murder that Wasn't

She caught Cathy on the back stairs and asked her what a school cleaning lady would be likely to wear.

"Oh, Lady Darriby-Jones, I have the very thing for you. If you could make your way to the first-floor storeroom, where we keep all the janitorial supplies, I can deck you out for the part in no time at all."

"Thank you, my dear. I tell you what, can you pop a suitable outfit on the bed in my room? I've got to meet with Smith in a moment and then there's a pink gin waiting for me in the bar."

"How will I know your size, milady? They come in three sizes for the ladies that clean."

"Well, can't you just guess? I'm a little larger than you, but not much." That statement wasn't strictly true. Lady Darriby-Jones had three inches in height on Cathy, but quite a few more inches of bust and waist, the latter partly disguised by the corset she wore. She would, however, leave the decision of dress size to another rather than admit to a slim, young and agile thing that she had anything to be envious about.

Besides, it would be dark and the disguise didn't need to fit exactly to convince the night porter, who Cathy informed her couldn't boast as to razor-sharp eyesight.

Three pink gins later, Smith held the door of the Rolls open to a remarkable sight wobbling across the driveway of the Auchin Hotel. Wrapped in a flower-patterned overall tied with a bow behind, her distinctive curly hairdo was covered in a matching triangle of cheap cloth fastened in an irritating-to-her manner beneath her chin. Beneath the overall, Lady Darriby-Jones had squeezed into the medium dress, a dull beige falling to mid-calf. She had only managed the seemingly impossible process of getting dressed, by tightening her corset beyond where she would normally go.

Beyond where any lady could reasonably to be called upon in the line of duty.

She had a particular problem in getting into the Rolls, not because of any restrictions on her legs, the dress and overalls having been designed with freedom of movement in mind. It was more a fear that the whole set-up would come undone with the slightest level of exertion beyond limited and slow movements; hardly conducive to her occupation as a cleaner, but there you have it.

In the end, although she wouldn't have chosen it this way, Smith gave her a shove and she sort of slid into place. At least getting out should be easier because of gravity.

"The school, as we discussed, Smith," Lady Darriby-Jones wheezed. Smith closed the door and went around to the driver's seat and prepared to drive off.

Then he mentioned two things that told Lady Darriby-Jones that he was thinking hard on her mission. The first was easy, the second harder to resolve.

"You'll need a name, milady. I mean, like a cleaner's name."

"Yes, what suggestion?" It really was difficult to talk with the corset so tight.

"Millie, I think." He slid the compartment divider back and handed her something on a pin. "I took the liberty of making you a name badge, milady, I mean Millie."

"Name badge?" Getting a whole sentence out seemed impossible.

"To pin on your overalls. Cathy said it would mean less questions asked. You see, how are you going to sound convincing, Millie?" He clearly rather enjoyed using the name he had chosen, the nearest he could come to 'milady'.

"What mean?"

"The accent, of course. You don't exactly sound convincing as a Scottish cleaner, although I must say you look the part!"

"Goodness," she hadn't thought of that. But Smith had.

"If you could give me the badge back a moment, Millie." He drew out his fountain pen and spent a full minute printing something on the homemade badge he and Cathy had put together while Lady Darriby-Jones was busy with her pink gins.

"Here," he said, handing it back. Lady Darriby-Jones switched the internal light on to see what he had added and would have laughed if it hadn't hurt so much:

Millie
Deaf and Dumb
But the Best Cleaner Ever

"Apparently, Millie, you're supplied by an agency that does this sort of thing, I mean package up young girls and ship them off to the school or other such places to mop, dust and scrub." Smith said, leaving Lady Darriby-Jones feeling rather uneasy at the hard labour stretching before her. She certainly felt packaged up and despatched as the car slid through the still night until it reached the old gatehouse to the school. "Best if you walk from here, Millie, as not many cleaners will be arriving in a Rolls Royce."

It wasn't a problem at all getting into the school; the cleaners came every evening as a team and worked till quite late to get the school sorted out in spick and span fashion, swept, dusted and polished, also emptying the bins and doing whatever was necessary following the mess of three hundred boys charging around the place. The night porter, a shrivelled man with a habit of opening and shutting his eyes constantly in an off-putting, fluttering motion, probably from some scare during the Great War, let her in with barely a word of enquiry. He read her name badge and deduced that she wasn't going to give an explanation as to why she was allocated to the school instead of the regular girl, not least because she was unable to.

"Welcome to Auchin School for Boys," he said, with a strong hint of sarcasm born of long service without recognition. "Welcome, Millie. Now, there's a lot to do tonight, so you better take this mop and start on the first floor."

She nodded her acceptance of her role and shambled off towards the main staircase, trying to act the part of yet another cleaner going about her every day duties.

"No, not that way. You see, the main stairs have already been cleaned and we don't want you messing them up, Millie. Take the back staircase, the one through there." As he spoke, he mimed the actions to her. "Yes, that's right. When you get up there, I want you to clean the whole floor and then dust everywhere. No, that's not right, silly me; dust first and then you can mop the floor."

When she climbed, somewhat awkwardly, up the steep steps, strained by the tightness of her corset and feeling very unfamiliar in her plain nylon rags, she realised that she had the whole of the first floor to herself.

"How wonderful," she muttered to herself, before realising that she shouldn't be talking, playing the role of a mute. But, she thought, I've got the cherry on the cake on top of all the icing. This is wonderful; the whole of the first floor and hours to search it. Now I wonder where Freddie could be.

She didn't have to wonder very long because Freddie appeared a moment later. First, she heard some clattering on the steps behind her, the ones she had just used. Recognising that she shouldn't be able to hear anything, being deaf as well as mute, she carried on with her work as if nothing was happening around her, swishing the duster the night porter given her this way and that, thinking there's nothing much to this cleaning lark.

"Hello, auntie," Freddie spoke in a loud voice. She turned, of course, and had to place two fingers on her lips to indicate silence.

"Oh," he said, half guessing the role she was playing, "you must be one of the new cleaners then. Are you filling in for Sally?"

Then he spotted her name badge, and it all made sense. "Oh, my dear, it must be so difficult not being able to talk or hear anything that's going on around. I've just come down here because the prefect sent me to collect some papers from the headmaster's study. Perhaps you could clean in there while I'm looking for the papers as I'm a bit scared with all the goings on around here in the dark, and with there being murders going on left right and centre. I say left right and centre but actually it's just one murder, that of our old headmaster, Mr Hardway. He was topped, or rather sliced up, in that very study I've got to go into and I'm really quite frightened of going in there on my own."

Of course, Lady Darriby-Jones heard everything, but had to pretend not to. Freddie, in response, took her arm and guided her towards the inner study, the room in which murder had been committed.

They just had no idea who by.

Lady Darriby-Jones had valid doubts about the other murders, strongly suspecting them to be non-murders, but this one had definitely taken place. Now, she had the chance to snoop about to her heart's content while her pyjama-clad nephew kept a lookout.

What she didn't count on was the self-installed new-but-old headmaster returning to his study barely a moment into her search for clues.

Chapter Fourteen

When you want to find something, the best place to look is the waste-paper basket belonging to the person you're investigating, at least according to Lady Darriby-Jones. She found this an increasingly unpleasant task, given a growing dependence on this new-fangled chewing gum, with the spent bits being discarded in other people's waste paper baskets, usually wrapped in a scrap of paper that needs to be unwrapped in case the selected scrap contained pertinent information.

She had intended to make straight for the waste-paper basket in the little study, not expecting to find anything concerning the murder (she sincerely hoped any such evidence had been catalogued and referenced by the police already), but she sought a clue or two as to why Major Blythe had stormed his way back into the school after the murder of Hardway and post his own retirement. However, at the moment she didn't dare move towards her target because of the impending presence of Major Blythe, moving through the outer office and towards the inner sanctuary. Both she and Freddie just had enough time to crouch down behind the desk. Hardly the best hiding place, but something at least. Freddie then decided that it was a distinctly inadequate hiding place. Looking wildly around, he indicated for a move across the open study floor to slot in behind the large sofa by the window, there being a gap behind where the curtains hung down to the ground. He indicated for Lady Darriby-Jones to follow him and, as a pair, they crawled on hands and knees across no man's land to the relative security of the narrow spot between the window and the sofa. They made it a second before the study door was flung open.

It's just as well they made the transfer because Major Blythe flicked the light on and moved straight to the desk, which he started rummaging through; they would have been directly in his path. Clearly looking for something, they could hear him becoming irritated by his lack of success.

Eventually, after pulling out all the drawers to the desk so they fell to the floor with a crash one after the other, he gave up on the desk.

At least he appeared to give up, because the next thing they knew, he had moved away from the desk and was pulling up the cushions of the sofa, inches from where Lady Darriby-Jones and Freddie lay in hiding. Finally, he sat down on the sofa, or rather collapsed into it with a cry of anguish. The movement of the sofa caused by his overlarge body caused some discomfort to Lady Darriby-Jones, hidden right behind where he now sat and not in the most comfortable of positions.

She had to hold her nerve, had to stay calm throughout the several minutes he sat there, not allowing herself even the tiniest movement lest it give their location to the enemy. She imagined events as they might turn out if she and Freddie were discovered by this plainly aggressive man.

Two aggressive headmasters, sandwiching a day's tenure with the gentle Mr Robertson. What attracted these aggressive fellows to lead a boy's boarding school?

Actually, it was a two-layered sandwich, for hadn't Hardway's period in office been both preceded and succeeded by this oaf, who also happened to be Freddie's uncle by dint of being the earl's younger brother? How could two brothers differ so much?

After five agonising minutes, Major Blythe seemed to decide that enough was enough and he left the study flicking the light switch as he departed, leaving them secure, uncomfortable and in total darkness. It was another three or four minutes before either Lady Darriby-Jones or Freddie dared to move.

"It seems our friend, Major Blythe, was looking for something, too." Lady Darriby-Jones hissed despite her mute state.

"Yes," said Freddie, "but what is it we're looking for?"

"I really don't know Freddie, my dear. I just know that there has to be some clue here, somewhere. If we can find something, we'll move the case along. Cathy spoke about some strange receipts, and I'm wondering if Major Blythe was after the same." She had a hunch, but it was just that, a hunch, and she wasn't going to get Freddie's hopes up just to dash them again. "We've got to keep looking and the first place I'm going to try, given that Major Blythe has looked through the drawers of the desk thoroughly, is it in the waste-paper basket."

She found it after 15 seconds bent over the selected object. There were only five or six pieces of paper in there and, after opening two of them to find nothing but doodles, presumably done and then discarded by Hardway on the afternoon of his murder, she came up trumps with the third scrap.

"Look," Lady Darriby-Jones said, "it seems to be directions taken over the phone and then screwed up and thrown in here. It might just fit with what Cathy said."

"Except it isn't complete," Freddie said, taking the paper and peering at it. "What good are half a set of directions and where do they lead to, anyway?"

Freddie was right, of course; they didn't even know whether these were the first half or the second half, just that they were obviously torn in several places, therefore a chunk was missing.

"Second right, straight for six miles, then left on the sharp bend into the wood. Keep going for four miles onto open ground and then turn..." Freddie read the words scrawled on the paper and scratched his head with both sets of fingers. It was a puzzle.

They checked the other papers in the bin but they were all doodles. Clearly Hardway had been a doodler, quite a good one too, making Lady Darriby-Jones think about how fascinating the construction of each human being was; they can be all over wicked but still have a talent that people would die for.

The trouble was that people were dying and she felt the responsibility to find out why.

They were about to leave, mission accomplished in Lady Darriby-Jones' opinion, when Freddie bent over the mess of papers from the drawers, dropped on the floor and started to scoop up armfuls of them.

"What are you doing?"

"We need a bag or something," Freddie replied, but no bag was to be found. In the end, without knowing Freddie's reasons for gathering great piles of papers, she found a way to improvise.

"Undo my overalls," she said to her nephew, turning around so he could tackle the bow at the back. "We can make a bag out of them."

An ingenious idea, but also one that was to put Lady Darriby-Jones in grave danger.

As she was about to find out.

"Right," said Lady Darriby-Jones, as Freddie hefted this awkward homemade bag onto his shoulder and made for the door, "you need to get back to bed."

"No way, aunty, not when the excitement's just starting."

But Lady Darriby-Jones was adamant. She had a strong impression of what Major Blythe would do to boys found outside the dorms at night, especially when slinking around the first floor where his study-suite was situated. And she certainly didn't want Freddie to be exposed to that terror.

Freddie put up a good fight, arguing that the bag was too heavy for Lady Darriby-Jones to carry. He was probably right about that, especially as the cleaning costume she was squeezed into made every movement awkward, in fact rendering it impossible to move quickly and with agility; she felt like a dumpy old cleaning lady, which said a lot about her ability to disguise herself.

It looked to be a stand-off with Freddie insisting on coming with her and Lady Darriby-Jones insisting that he stay behind, safe and sound. It became a battle of wills and Lady Darriby-Jones won, but only just, Freddie finally acknowledging that it was safer for him to be dorm-bound rather than making for freedom in the great outdoors.

"Your uncle is probably still around right now. I doubt very much that he's crept off to his own bed with so much bothering him. If he joins a few of the dots, it will lead straight to you, Freddie, and that's not a risk I'm ready to take."

They made their way down the corridor, around the main stairs in the centre of the building and back towards the back staircase that Lady Darriby-Jones had climbed up from the ground floor, while Freddie had descended from the floor above where the dorms were situated.

"Freddie, my dear, you must go up to your dorm now and I'll be fine from here. I'll just go down the stairs and out through the front door and I'll be away. Smith will be waiting for me just outside. The car's parked at the gatehouse but he walked up the drive with me earlier."

As she turned to go down the stairs, Freddie passed the makeshift bag to her and the change in weight distribution on a finely balanced structure caused her to stumble right on the first step. Freddie, perhaps seeing a glimmer of hope, as well as a jolt of concern for his aunt, steadied her quickly, and then came up with an idea.

"Why don't you put the bag in the dumbwaiter?" he said, "I'm sure it still works."

"Good idea, Freddie." She pulled the door open just as they heard a sound of footsteps on the floor above. "It must be your uncle," she said. "Go quickly, Freddie, you don't want to be found out of bed in the middle of the night."

Now that he faced imminent discovery, his courage failed him, but not before one last attempt to stay with his beloved aunt.

"Are you sure, aunty?"

"Absolutely sure, Freddie, go now."

After he had leapt up the stairs, Lady Darriby-Jones paused a while, leaning on the open hatch of the dumbwaiter, feeling pretty exhausted with so much going on; nervous exhaustion, she thought, could be every bit as shattering as the physical variety.

She leant back a little further, trying to ease the load of the makeshift bag stuffed full of papers that meant nothing to her.

That's how it happened, something to do with physics, although Lady Darriby-Jones would later put it down to fate, not having much of a concept of the workings of physics.

She leant back and toppled in the same direction. It was neat and precise. Her legs flew up and followed her torso into the dumbwaiter. She remembered hearing footsteps coming down the back stairs; no voices, so presumably Freddie had got away back to the dorm without being caught. That was good news.

But not such good news for what was happening in her immediate world. The weight of her body, combined with the 'overall bag' was too much for the worn-out ropes on the dumbwaiter, or at least too much for the braking system of counter weights. The platform fell to the ground floor, accelerating as it went past the ground floor and shuddering to a halt in the basement, winding her in the process.

When she got her breath back, she tried to climb out of the dumbwaiter but could not make it; she struggled and struggled, but finally had to admit defeat. She was stuck until someone found her and could drag her out by her feet.

So close to getting away, but a miss is as good as a mile.

Chapter Fifteen

She slept there, in the bottom of the dumbwaiter, upside down with her legs folded in on top of her.

She slept in a manner of speaking, for she woke every few minutes, whether from fear, cold or discomfort. With no way to tell the time, she lacked even the knowledge that in so many hours she would be discovered and dragged before Major Blythe, the king in his own little kingdom.

She slept, yes, but never came close to reviving her sagging spirit, knowing that, at some time in the future, she would be found in this heap; how could she hope for even a scrap of dignity?

Then, darker thoughts moved in. What if she was never found? What if this part of the kitchen was not used anymore? Would someone, in years to come, find a pile of bones amidst the remnants of hundreds of pieces of paper? Would a later day sleuth scratch their head over the Mystery of the Bag of Bones, before remembering that once, long ago, a certain aristocratic lady had disappeared?

. . .

What she didn't know, indeed, how could she, was that the night porter was both lazy and a man of habit; the type who would send the sentries around the castle walls to exactly the same schedule every night, making it easy for the attacking force to scale the walls at the right moment and knock off each slow-witted guard one at a time. Having never read a comic book in her life, how could she know that this was precisely how the story went at that stage?

She didn't know then, but it was all to come out, fully detailed and explained to her by unfolding events.

The night porter was lazy. Of his ten-hour shift, he worked hard for two or three hours at the front end, mainly getting the cleaners organised, and aware that some of the teachers would still be around in the latter stages of the evening. Then, he would retire to his cubby-hole and settle down with some of the Scotch he pinched on a regular basis from the locked cupboard in the staff room. Every glass he poured involved a ritual of self-congratulation. He had long ago duplicated the key held by one of the staff members designated with responsibility for the drinks cabinet, and added water in case someone was monitoring the level in each bottle.

Long practice had shown him the exact amount of whisky required each night to dull the pain from the wound in his leg, without (a) making him too sleepy that he failed in his early morning duties or (b) generating a maudlin mood as he relived the trenches and the way the shell casing had ripped into him, destroying much of the function of his right leg.

That dose was three glasses neat, no water to dilute it, no ice to cool it, just as God and man made it, for there was the work of God in the making of any bottle of Scotch.

Then, at precisely 5am, he would rise from his semi-slumber, put the bottle and glass away and resume his duties, as if he had been at it all night long. The evening shift varied with the quality of the cleaners the agency sent, but there was a sweetness to the early morning session because it followed an exact routine every time.

He started with the dorms at the top of the building, flashing his torch into each one to ensure no disturbance during the night, nothing out of the usual. Then, he trod the main stairs down to the first floor where the offices were and the live-in teachers' bedrooms. Then the ground floor, dominated by classrooms and changing rooms, finally the basement with kitchens and refectory, where three-hundred boys gathered to eat three times a day.

That morning was no different, at least not yet as he shuffled down the back stairs to the kitchen. The only irritation was that the new cleaner assigned to the first floor, didn't seem to have lifted a finger. It was no good. She would have to go. Her lack of hearing and inability to talk didn't give her an adequate excuse for not doing the work with diligence. He would write a note to the agency about it.

He always checked the refectory first, with good reason. Leaving the kitchen to last meant the undercook would have arrived by the time he was concluding his tour of inspection. He liked the undercook with her pert and petite body and her twinkling eyes; he wondered, as she quickly rustled up eggs and bacon for him, whether he had a chance with her. Each morning, his courage deserted him and he set a fresh challenge for the next time.

Funny, Lady Darriby-Jones later reflected, how a man like the night porter can face down machine gun fire and win a medal for saving his sergeant's life, suffering the mutilation of his own leg in the process, yet can't find the nerve to ask a young undercook for a date.

It was, without doubt, a strange world where coincidences combined with incidental incidences in a great big mash of fun and games in which nothing was fair, nothing worked out like the cheap detective novels she consumed by the shelf-full, yet her world remained wonderful and charming in the extreme.

Witnessed by her rescue from a potentially embarrassing and awkward-to-explain position head over heels in a dumbwaiter for the night.

Or was that heels over head?

She first heard his voice, and fear gripped her. This was the moment of reckoning, of discovery and humiliation.

"Well, good God, what have we here?" She recognised the voice from the evening before. "I do believe it's a body piled in there, or at least the bottom half."

Lady Darriby-Jones tensed as two hands gripped her ankles and tugged, then paused and tugged again. "It's no good. I can't get purchase with this damned leg of mine." Then there was a shuffling, leg-dragging sound as the night porter moved on.

The Mystery of the Murder that Wasn't

Had the man given up? Two half-hearted attempts at dragging her out of her predicament, and that was that? She strained to hear something in the silence, nothing but a slight scrabbling noise right behind her head. Something was moving within the dumb waiter.

It was a rat. She screamed, remembered her mute status, then shrugged and screamed again. The rat came around to the front, facing her directly, its eyes shining through the dark, its teeth visible when it twitched its mouth open. It looked to her as if it was getting ready to take a bite from her cheek, relishing the thought of that soft, tasty flesh.

She screamed again when two sets of hands grabbed her ankles. A girl's voice cried, 'on three, three', giggling at her little joke. Lady Darriby-Jones then felt powerful forces yanking her back out of the dumbwaiter and to freedom, or relative freedom.

The last thing she saw was the rat slinking away, an opportunity lost, but there would be others.

The force of the pull was sufficient to get her right out of the dumbwaiter. Moreover, it landed her on top of those pulling, to make a tangled heap on the floor of the corridor right outside the kitchen. She felt two warm bodies moving beneath her and strove to extricate herself so that her saviours might live and breathe again. Slowly, she managed the task, standing stiffly in the corridor and lending a hand to the first fallen figure.

Who happened to be the undercook. After straightening herself out, the two of them managed to pull on the night porter, also bringing him to the upright.

Three bodies dusting themselves down and testing every limb for damage. Unfortunately, when the night porter tested his right leg, which normally could take some weight, it gave way immediately and he ended up on the floor.

"Oh, Robbie," the undercook cried, "I don't want to lose you." The undercook crouched down to be with him.

"It's the leg playing up again," Robbie replied. "You haven't lost me, Fiona."

"I know just the thing," Fiona said, "bacon and eggs with Scotch milk in yer tea." She looked up at Lady Darriby-Jones, saw, no doubt, a dishevelled and broken domestic close to tears, "It looks like your lady friend could do with a similar revival."

The whole story came out over an early breakfast for four, Lady Darriby-Jones insisting that she be allowed to fetch Smith from outside where he had been patiently waiting all night, pacing the lower reaches of the drive and despairing of ever seeing his employer again.

"So, you're not a dumb mute?" the night porter asked, recognising the obvious because Lady Darriby-Jones had quite a lot to say.

"No, Mr Grant, I'm not. I'm afraid the dumb waiter put paid to my disguise as a dumb mute."

"Very good, miss, dumb waiter and dumb mute. But, you're not a cleaner either, are you? Your accent alone..."

"No, I'm Lady Darriby-Jones, a relative of Freddie Blythe, who's a pupil here."

"A lovely lad too," Fiona MacIntosh said. "He's often around the kitchens seeking a nibble or two, such a cheery chap."

"That sounds like Freddie."

"But why, milady?" the night porter asked, "I mean why dress up as a cleaner and come in to the school at night?"

Lady Darriby-Jones looked at Smith before replying, seeking assurance from one of the team. He nodded ever so slightly, getting the meaning of her look.

"It's a long story."

"We've got an hour until anybody else comes in," Fiona replied, "although I'll need to get on with breakfast for the masses and I'm behind already."

"We'll all help with brekkie while I tell you what's being going on," Lady Darriby-Jones suggested; after all, she had experience as a cleaning maid, so why not try out kitchen work too?

And that's exactly what they did, piling up toast and stirring a great vat of porridge.

"How much tea can three-hundred boys drink?" Smith asked as he heaved another giant urn into place.

"You'll be surprised," Fiona replied. Then she stopped her work at the stove for a minute, processing what Lady Darriby-Jones had been telling her. "I do believe I may be able to help in your investigation, Lady Darriby-Jones."

"How might that be, my dear?"

"Well, I'm only undercook, so don't get too involved in the money side of running the kitchens here, but I've long suspected some money being scraped off the top, if you get my drift."

"You mean?"

"Exactly, Lady Darriby-Jones, you see this breakfast, for instance. It consists of porridge and toast with jam, washed down with cups of tea and plenty of sugar."

"Yes, what of it? Are you thinking it a bit light on the nourishment scale?"

"Come and see this," she led Lady Darriby-Jones and the other two into a small office, probably once the butler's pantry, where she pulled out a book. "This is the meal book, dictating what food is served. A lot of it is dedicated to lunch and supper, but this first section deals with breakfast."

Lady Darriby-Jones read the entry:

"Breakfast fundamentally consists of porridge and toast with one of the following added each day," she paused, her eyes had taken her further along the line so that she had a head start on the others for realisation, "kippers, kedgeree, eggs and bacon."

"There's none of that," Robbie Grant, the night porter at the school, said with the indignance and outrage of someone who had cheated others himself, witness the whisky levels in the staff room.

"Nor the orange juice that's being given twice a week, plus on Sundays."

. . .

Lady Darriby-Jones felt a sudden longing for her bed as Smith and she left her new friends in the kitchen; night porter and undercook were busy planning their evening at the pictures on Robbie's next night off. Lady Darriby-Jones knew that, however exhausted she might be from her night time excursions in disguise, there was no time for rest because the undercook's suspicions added yet another dimension to this mystery.

And, somehow, she had to find solutions.

Chapter Sixteen

Once outside, still and dark in the early morning of a Highland winter, Lady Darriby-Jones asked Smith whether he was up to a drive that day, knowing that he would do whatever job she asked of him, but seriously concerned because he had been awake all night waiting for her return; the strain on him in recent days amounted to severe on the weather scale and she didn't want to put more upon him.

He replied that he still had a lot left to give and they spent the walk back to the car deciding on the best route because she had two immediate objectives, both of which she felt would be better carried out that day.

"First," she said, "I really think we need to pay Mr Robertson a visit in the prison in Inverness, just to see how he's getting on." She didn't mention that she also wanted to question Mr Robertson on two fronts, those being whether he had any connections with Alfie when at Oxford, and how on earth Major Blythe had marched in there and stripped him of his position.

"Yes, milady," Smith replied, "I think that an excellent idea as it will be an incredible shock for him to be incarcerated, especially from his middle-class background. Perhaps we can take Lady Alice and Mr Burrows so that he can have some company his own age."

"Yes, good idea, Smith. Now the second thing is that we need to go over to the Blythe country seat at Cosforth and see what, if any, clues we can pick up there. I'm really having second thoughts about whether the earl and countess have been murdered or whether they're just been taken out of action for the time being."

They decided on the prison first; the twenty-six miles down to Inverness would take them an hour but Smith had heard it was then a pleasant drive up the coast to the Blythe country seat at Cosforth.

"With a fair wind behind us, Smith, we'll be back at Auchin in time for a nap after lunch." Did she sound convincing enough?

They arrived back at the hotel to find Alfie downstairs eating breakfast and Lady Alice was nowhere to be seen. After briefing Alfie on the goings on that night, Lady Darriby-Jones left to rouse her daughter, while Smith continued to brief Alfie on the events they planned for that day. After shaking the old sleepyhead several times, Lady Darriby-Jones managed to get her awake sufficiently to conduct a similar exercise while Lady Alice dressed in grumpy fashion.

Just off the Old Edinburgh Road, Porterfield Prison in Inverness, boasted two things. It was of modern construction, built at the turn of the century to modern standards. Secondly, it was tiny. The governor, who met Lady Darriby-Jones and the others at the reception area, informed them that it held a maximum of a hundred-and-two prisoners, "mostly male but with a contingent of lady prisoners as well."

"You have both?"

"Needs must, Lady Darriby-Jones. I don't know whether us Highlanders are more law-abiding or better at getting away with it, but this is the only prison for the entire region and it doesn't warrant separate establishments for each gender."

"Yes, of course, Mr Cameron, now, our interest is a young gentleman held here on remand, a Mr Robertson, who..."

"Mr Robertson, you say? Goodness me, quite a personality. He's certainly a live wire!"

"Really?" Lady Darriby-Jones was brought to a stop, literally, such that Alfie, following behind, almost ran into the back of her.

'Yes, really," the governor replied, his face unable to hide his grin, "he's got the whole prison going with his education drive. I hate to wish ill of any living person, but a part of me hopes he'll be in for a long stretch. He's a natural leader of men, no doubt about that. Ask Fraser, here, he's the senior prison officer, actually been here since the prison opened in 1902, longer than most inmates, I'm sure, eh, Fraser?"

"Indeed, sir, longer than any of them, sir."

"Tell Lady Darriby-Jones and the others in her party about the impact Robertson has made since coming to us, what, just a few days ago, I believe."

"That's right, sir, it's amazing what he's done in a few short days. He's rejuvenated the whole education programme, Lady eh..."

"Darriby-Jones, Mr Fraser." Lady Darriby-Jones was intrigued to find out more. "So, what has he done to turn the place upside down?"

"Sad to say, Lady Darriby-Jones, he's created something from nothing. By that, I mean there never was even a half-decent education programme before he arrived. Now, he's somehow managed to inspire just about everyone to start studying. Some are following practical subjects such as carpentry and plumbing. A few have taken law books out of the library, while half-a-dozen have started Latin, that being Mr Robertson's particular subject."

"Several have taken up mathematics, four are in Mr Robertson's Spanish class and we even have someone studying chemistry, about which Mr Robertson informs me he knows nothing at all," Mr Cameron added, as if Fraser's praise needed any endorsement.

"So, would it be fair to say that Mr Robertson has settled in satisfactorily, Mr Fraser?" Lady Alice asked.

"Yes, miss, eh, milady," Fraser replied, blushing slightly at being addressed by such an elegant and imposing aristocratic figure, "he's settled in just perfectly, although, of course, he maintains his innocence."

"Don't they all, Mr Fraser?" Smith asked, trailing the others very slightly but definitely feeling part of the band of detectives.

"As a rule, yes, you happen to be dead right there, sir, and, in my time, I've seen thousands of declarations of innocence that I know to be complete untruths. But, with Robertson, well, it's different somehow."

Discussion of the innocence or guilt of the 'headmaster-for-a-day' reminded Lady Darriby-Jones that she needed to quiz Mr Robertson on a few matters, rather than just ponder on the wonders of a world where an unassuming bod like Mr Robertson could have such hidden skills and capabilities.

She suggested they catch up with Mr Robertson. The governor hastily complied, "provided," he said, "that it doesn't interrupt his lessons. We wouldn't want to risk that, you know."

They met Mr Robertson in the visitors' room, deserted now because it fell outside regular visiting hours.

"Mr Robertson, how good it is to see you. Are they looking after you such that you're keeping well?" Lady Darriby-Jones started the catch-up.

"Yes, excellent care, no complaints at all," he replied, giving a boyish grin.

"We've heard great things about you," Lady Alice said, moving the conversation along in neat little increments.

"There's a lot to do in here. Grub's not bad, either, better than school at any rate!"

"Mr Robertson," Lady Darriby-Jones said, "I want to ask you about your time at Oxford, specifically whether you knew this man," she stepped aside to reveal Alfie, who she had deliberately been keeping behind her. She watched his face intently, looking for signs of recognition, but none came her way.

"No, Lady Darriby-Jones, apart from seeing Mr... Burrows in school the other day, I've never seen him before."

Lady Alice had been briefed to watch Alfie's face for similar signs and reported shortly afterwards that Alfie had been telling the truth when he had denied any prior knowledge of Mr Robertson.

Deep down, Lady Darriby-Jones knew that, but it was gratifying to have her belief in Alfie demonstrated.

"Good," she said, "now, the next thing, Mr Robertson, is to understand fully and absolutely what happened when Major Blythe usurped you, taking back the role of headmaster he had relinquished barely a year ago."

"Well, that I believe I can be more of a help on, Lady Darriby-Jones, as the events are forever seared into my memory."

A spotty youth moved into the room at that moment, carrying a tray of coffee cups as well as a huge coffee pot.

"Mr Fraser said ta bring this in," the prisoner said, his distinct Glaswegian accent being almost unintelligible to those from south of the border. "Shall I be Ma'am? Good, well you're chatting to a saint, ladies and gents. Robertson only set the whole prison alive with his education drive. Why, I dropped out of school when I was eleven, got into a gang running stolen property here in the Highlands down to the rich fellahs back hame. Then got sent here for me sins."

"What's Mr Robertson done, lad, that you enthuse about him so energetically?" Lady Alice asked out of genuine interest, wanting to hear it from the horse's mouth.

"Why, he's got us all set up with learnin' things. I'm gonna get me exams and go ta university, that's me sorted out."

"Thank you, lad. I'm so glad you found your way in life and wish you all the success in the world when you get out." The contrast between Lady Alice's languid elegance and the brusque street language of the boy stood out for all to see, but the appreciation of Mr Robertson was common to both. Lady Darriby-Jones also noted the contrast between Lady Alice's forthright and open words and the sultry tones she had employed ever since she had arrived at Inverness Station. There was a deal of sorting out that she had to do with her daughter, but that would have to wait for calmer times.

The lad reluctantly departed after pouring several cups and making a complete hash of it. Everybody's attention turned back to Mr Robertson. He glugged down his coffee, "the first decent cup I've had since I arrived here," and cleared his throat, intent upon spelling out the strange actions that led him to the shortest ever reign as a headmaster in any school ever.

And what he told his audience of four amazed everyone collected there, most especially his opening sentence.

Chapter Seventeen

"I'm not a teacher at all," he said.

"What?"

"I'm a copper, an undercover police detective."

"What?" Lady Darriby-Jones repeated, unable to take it in.

"But why are you in prison, then?" Alfie asked, gathering his wits before the others could, seeing the gross incongruity of the situation.

"So as not to break my cover," he replied, then thought his audience deserved a better explanation.

"We suspected Hardway of syphoning funds from the school."

"I knew it. As soon as I heard their food was not up to par, I suspected someone was pinching the food kitty."

"You're right, Lady Darriby-Jones, but it went deeper than that. We believe he was skimming money from the fees, overcharging through a dodgy building maintenance firm and following another dozen 'get rich at someone else's expense' ploys, including the kitchen debacle. I was assigned to go undercover and find out exactly what was going on. And, believe me, there was plenty."

"Why didn't you move in, then?" Lady Alice, probably the most cynical of them all, asked. Lady Darriby-Jones considered it an excellent question, one that had been on the tip of her own tongue.

"Because we kept finding more schemes, or rather I found them and reported back to the chief super here in Inverness."

That put it in context, Lady Darriby-Jones thought, who this mysterious undercover operative reported to and who, presumably, was the mastermind behind the investigation into corruption.

Moreover, she understood (a) why the chief super had not deemed it fit to tell her (on the basis that the less people who knew the better) and (b) why he wanted to get Mr Robertson out of the way temporarily when the misdemeanour list grew suddenly to encompass murder.

"And then Hardway suddenly dies, several knife thrusts and a slit throat to make sure," she said, probing her way, but making progress; her mind working at lightning speed as jigsaw pieces flew together, several blocks at a time.

"Yes, that threw a complete spanner in the works," Mr Robertson said, although that wouldn't be his real name. "The powers that be decided that I had to get out pronto and what better way than to be arrested and spend a few weeks as a guest of His Majesty."

The Mystery of the Murder that Wasn't

"Clever," said Lady Darriby-Jones as she cycled a thousand thoughts through her head. "It answers some of the questions but creates a whole load more."

"Like, who killed Hardway? The other advantage of arresting me is that we thought the real culprit would get careless, thinking he's off the hook. He might even know about the corruption and believe he can muscle in and help himself to Hardway's ill-gotten gains. In fact, the pile of cash was a possible motive for the murder."

"Major Blythe came into the inner study last night, searching desperately for something." But something didn't sit quite right. It's a huge leap from theft to murder, especially a murder of passion, strictly several of them with the earl and countess being declared dead too.

"How do you know this?" Mr Robertson asked, so Lady Darriby-Jones gave him a rundown on the events of last night, going light on the 'stuck in the dumb waiter' bit for obvious reasons when she got to that part of her narrative.

"I was stuck but the night porter, Mr Grant, helped me out and that's when Fiona, the undercook, told me about the meal skimping. That's when I started to suspect theft from the school."

"Grant, you say?" Mr Robertson picked up on the name immediately. "He's one of the main suspects, either for the thieving, as an associate to Hardway, or possibly the murder."

"Could it be both?" Alfie asked. "Look at it like this. He was an associate of Hardway and fell out with him because Hardway was trying to cheat him out of his share of the proceeds. They have it out in Hardway's study and, suddenly, there's a body just lying there."

"No, Mr Grant wouldn't do such a thing."

"Well, he steals whisky from the staff room. I've seen his do that a dozen times over the year I've been there."

"Yes, well, that's probably medicinal, wonky leg, you know, from the war." Having benefitted from his chivalry, of sorts, and seen the softer side of him in relation to Fiona, Lady Darriby-Jones found it hard to suspect the night porter of anything. She stood up, needing to get away, needing to sort through a thousand conflicting thoughts.

"When will you get out?" Smith asked, changing the subject and, thus, adding another dimension to the puzzle that was becoming more complex by the minute.

"Out of here? That's the downside, because I can't be released just yet, not until the real murderer has been caught. Or at least until he makes a mistake that we notice so we can then jump on him."

"I... we've got to go, Mr Robertson, we'll come back soon, if you don't mind. It's just that..."

"I know it's a lot to take in, Lady Darriby-Jones. Just bear one thing in mind as you push these ideas through your head."

"That the two crimes may not be connected."

"Spot on, Lady Darriby-Jones, the chief super said you were bright as a button, if you don't think me cheeky in mentioning it; apparently, he had a long chat with the chief

The Mystery of the Murder that Wasn't

constable down your way. Well, in my old haunt, actually, when I was at Oxford."

Far from thinking it a cheek, Lady Darriby-Jones' cheeks flushed with pride as she and the others left the prison and walked back to her car.

She was getting a reputation; soon they would be writing detective books about her.

Then she came down to earth with a bump; she still had to solve the mystery and all the reputation in the world wouldn't protect her from a failure on that front.

Lady Darriby-Jones spent the next forty-five minutes in total silence. In fact, she led the way in this regard, as nobody else felt like filling the silence. Lady Alice tried the once, with a 'Ho-Hum' contribution that was met with continued silence. After that, she tried no more.

Smith spoke next, and only to inform the three of them in the back that they were approaching Cosforth Castle. It wasn't a castle at all, although some Blythe at some stage had added a square tower with battlements, but also with large plate glass windows, making it totally impracticable in a siege.

But it was the most beautiful house in the most beautiful setting that Lady Darriby-Jones had ever seen, with thick woods behind and a gradual long descent to the sea in front. The house had everything; grand facades yet poky turrets and little, jutting-out rooves, large picture windows besides tiny medieval ones and grey granite mixing with brick.

This was Freddie's home, the place he pictured when he thought of his mother and father.

Normally, with the developing friendship between them, based on their family ties, the Darriby-Joneses would expect to be invited there; Darriby had come often as a boy, but had drifted apart in early adulthood before reforming the friendship in recent years. Yet Lady Darriby-Jones had never seen the place before. Smith, sensing this, or waiting for precise directions as to where to go, stopped just inside the tree line and turned the engine off for a moment; thus, they could drink in the beauty of Cosforth Castle together.

"Right, what now?" said Lady Alice, the first to finish her drinking in the beauty exercise.

"Drive around the back, please, Smith." Lady Darriby-Jones was second in the recovery stakes, forming a plan from nothing.

The main purpose of their plan, of course, was to poke their noses in and see what they could discover.

"The house is completely boarded up," Alfie said as they approached down a winding road between boulders, large mounds of tufty grass and fallen trees, as well as those not toppled by recent storms.

There was an air of neglect about the place; like a scene for a horror story, where the idyllic turned, by degrees, into the horrific, yet all opportunity to turn back and get the hell out of there denied one.

"Drive closer, but keep out of sight as long as possible," came the next order from Lady Darriby-Jones. Smith had volunteered during the war but had been too old to

The Mystery of the Murder that Wasn't

fight; recognising his ability, they gave him a role behind the wheel, driving a general who had been one of the more daring of the breed, regularly requiring Smith to drive into areas of heavy shelling for observation purposes.

That's how he later told Lady Darriby-Jones that he felt at that moment; trying to bolt from cover to cover in his staff car, aware that at any moment he could be no more.

They did make it down without being shelled and drove up to the side of the house where Smith parked the car and they all got out, an eerie silence descending as the engine cut to nothing.

"What's that smell?" Lady Alice said, sniffing the air.

"It's fire," Alfie said, sniffing the same air, until Lady Alice turned her back on him and sniffed a separate block. A mother's instinct told her to intervene in their lingering tiff, but she had bigger fish to fry that afternoon, or at least fish from a different pond.

On confirming it to be smoke in the air, Lady Darriby-Jones immediately thought of a house fire, perhaps in vengeance or maybe to destroy evidence. The thought of such a beautiful pile going up in flames made her want to cry as she concentrated on a thin column of smoke coming from the back of the house.

They walked around from the side to the back, drawn by the column of smoke as it if were a winch winding them steadily in. They kept a sharp lookout and received the reward as soon as they entered the kitchen garden, seeing an old man standing where the garden gave way to the orchard. A large dustbin from which the fire gave off varying colours and sparks seemed to occupy his full attention.

"What's he doing?" Alfie asked.

"Burning things," Lady Alice condescended to answer with a statement of the obvious.

"I know that, but..."

"But burning what?" Lady Darriby-Jones said, the tones of her voice pleading for concentration on the question at hand, rather than continuing the great war between the young couple.

"There's only one way to find out, milady." Smith was right and there seemed a path from their current position at the corner of the house to a spot much closer.

"Let's go then," she said, feeling every inch the soldier commanding a small troop deep behind enemy lines, wishing Freddie were here to enjoy the mission, then thinking how sad he would be to see his once lively house shut and boarded up.

No, on balance, best if Freddie was not here with them today.

They crept forward by crouching amongst the shrubs, causing considerable cramping-type pains in Lady Darriby-Jones' already challenged legs.

But she made it, because she had to. She would be a contender, she told herself as a particular bolt of pain travelled up her left leg, for the 'tough old nut of the year' prize.

The Mystery of the Murder that Wasn't

Except she could do with a little less of the 'old'.

She stopped at a large rosemary bush, flagging down her troop in true military style, maybe thirty yards from the target.

The figure at the dustbin looked familiar, yet she couldn't place him. Dressed in overlarge overalls, hanging from his large frame, they obscured much of the shape of his body; but it was the posture that gave him away, stooped as if embarrassed at his height, yet somehow also ramrod straight.

Who was the old man burning papers in a dustbin? She felt, if she could answer that, much of the mystery would fall into place. Only, she couldn't think where she had seen that stance before.

Chapter Eighteen

The dog came from nowhere. Not a big dog with a powerful jaw, but they often say the smaller ones are the fiercest, and this one, a terrier, proved the point.

"Who's there?" the old man cried when the yapper kicked up a stink, going for the lower regions of Lady Darriby-Jones' skirt, around about the shins; perhaps not the juiciest part of the human anatomy.

After the vicious attack on Lady Darriby-Jones, the dog turned its attention on Lady Alice, seeming to prefer her higher hemline with the resultant greater degree of leg exposed. Perhaps the terriers, as a breed, preferred bare flesh to mouthfuls of wool, but this particular dog had found a sweet spot and wouldn't let go of Lady Alice, causing her to hop about the place in anguish.

Alfie sprang into action. Whipping his braces from his trousers, after hastily discarding both jacket and pullover, he fastened one end around the dog's collar, managed to restrain the creature by pulling hard, then attached the other end to a nearby metal fence post. The dog didn't give up immediately or easily, Alfie's braces proving to be remarkably elastic giving the dog considerable scope to launch attacks at whoever came close, but eventually the combined strength of Alfie and Smith managed to get some form of control over her by winding the braces several times around the metal post to shorten the dog's range.

There was still the problem of the old man moving towards them with a crosspiece of the broken metal fence in his hands and calling out for whoever was there to show themselves.

For an old man, he seemed to be moving remarkably quickly, looming up on them at a pretty terrific pace. Alfie looked at Lady Alice and Lady Darriby-Jones looked towards Smith and, with no further communication, they retreated silently around the corner of the building, at which point they started to run. The old man must have reached the dog and released him, for just as they approached the car, the dog came yapping at their heels once more, this time picking on Lady Darriby-Jones, the slowest of the runners.

Back at the car they tumbled in, Smith starting the engine and driving at top speed, most doors still open as they swung around the front of the house, up the main drive and away. By looking behind, they could see the old man on the front drive shaking his metal post so that the dog kept jumping to try to catch it, no doubt thinking this a fine new game, although not as good as a couple of sets of aristocratic calves between the teeth.

They had seen what they needed to see. Lady Darriby-Jones had no idea who the old man was, although he looked painfully familiar.

It's just that so many people rang bells in Lady Darriby-Jones' memory bank; how was she supposed to recall each and every one?

It wasn't a long drive back to Auchin but halfway through the journey, as they crossed a high and desolate moor situated like a resting point for climbers before they got into the mountains proper, Lady Darriby-Jones asked Smith to stop the car so that they could get some fresh air.

"I find fresh air so helpful," she said. "Won't you get out, Alfie?" the others had tumbled out to calm their battered nerves by drinking in the cold moorland air.

"I would, Lady Darriby-Jones, but I can't." He indicated that his lack of braces presented a problem.

"You saved me, at the expense of your braces," Lady Alice said, sliding back into the car to be with her new hero. All traces of disdain and arrogance vanished.

"Let's go for a little walk," Lady Darriby-Jones said to Smith, meaning to give the younger generation a bit of space.

They walked through partly snow-covered heather for ten minutes, in no particular direction other than away from the road. It was early afternoon, but the day already looked ready to give up, despite the lack of clouds, suggesting a cold night waiting in the wings. They talked about the weather, about Mrs Smith and even a little about Darriby, before slipping back to the questions surrounding their mystery.

"The mystery of the murder that wasn't," said Lady Darriby-Jones suddenly.

"I don't follow you, milady."

"The mystery of the murder that wasn't," she repeated, just louder, following that ancient rule that confused meaning with hearing; the rule declared that if someone professed a lack of understanding, they just needed the subject matter repeated at a considerably increased volume.

And Lady Darriby-Jones never had a problem with explaining herself in this manner.

"No, I mean, why wasn't there a murder, milady?"

"There was, but also there wasn't." Lady Darriby-Jones was reacting to Smith's input to the conversation, but almost by rote, her thoughts on a different plane altogether.

Smith shrugged and wondered when they would return to the car, feeling the icy-cold of a descending January night in the Highlands and thinking longingly of the warm fireplaces dotted throughout the Auchin Hotel.

"It would be miserable to be out here without a fire at night," he said.

"What was that, Smith?"

"I just said... is that a building over there?" He pointed across the stark moorland to the west, where he could see the Grampian Mountains rising one after another until they melted into the horizon.

"I left my spectacles in the car," Lady Darriby-Jones replied, "I expect there are shepherd's huts or forestry buildings dotted around the place, but nobody will live up here, not in winter at any rate."

"I believe there's smoke rising from the hut, milady." Smith was peering towards something Lady Darriby-Jones could not even make out.

"Maybe they're a group of walkers out traversing the bens and glens of bonnie Scotland," she said, her mind concentrating on other things, like where she had seen the old man before.

"I do believe it must be time to get back, milady." Smith was right, jolting Lady Darriby-Jones from her contemplation, bringing her back to the reality of the night descending in the Highlands.

"Yes," she said, "lead on, Smith, I'm not actually certain of which way we came."

Smith was a good chauffeur, not just a steady and careful driver, but also with an excellent sense of direction; it wasn't a problem for him to turn the twosome around in the near-dark and lead the way back to the car, actually taking a short-cut so that they arrived back a little less than ten minutes later.

"Let's look at this methodically," Lady Darriby-Jones said to Smith when seated around a warming fire in the snug. Lady Alice sat separately with Alfie, suitably re-rigged with a fresh pair of braces. They seemed lost to the wider world, staring into each other's eyes like lovestruck teenagers in a scene you might see at the picture house.

Well, thought Lady Darriby-Jones, Ali was a teenager, not yet turned twenty, while Alfie wasn't much older. She was just pleased that the rift had passed over like clouds driven from the sky.

However, their absence from the meeting she had called put extra emphasis on Smith, who clearly felt the pressure. Whether he had chosen his lifestyle, or whether it had been thrust upon him, his bent was not one that called for the grey matter to be exercised on a regular basis.

Except it bothered him that smoke had been rising from the hut in the middle of nowhere. Just as it bothered Lady Darriby-Jones that she had seen the figure in the garden at Cosforth Castle before, just not dressed as a janitor going about janitorial duties.

"Younger perhaps," she said.

"Where would they get the fuel for the fire?" he said, but not in reply.

"But why make yourself older deliberately?"

"There's not a tree for miles around."

"Unless you're up to no good, of course."

"Perhaps they had it delivered, the wood, I mean."

"Where's Cathy?" Lady Darriby-Jones' voice moved up several degrees on the urgency scale, making Smith jump out from his ponderings.

"She must be at work at the school, milady, in which case she'll be back soon." He rose and declared he would find out, returning a neat five-minutes later with Cathy in tow.

"Ah, Cathy, did you manage to get the receipts, I mean the questionable ones?"

"I looked and someone got there before me, milady. The folder was empty. Moreover, a lot more was missing from several cabinets in the accounts office."

"Blow and blow again." Those were sharp words coming from Lady Darriby-Jones, who had been brought up never to let loose with profanity, her mother teaching her that, when tempted, she should substitute a harmless word and give full force to that. "There must be some connection."

"But I did find this," Cathy continued, her green eyes shining in excitement as she pulled a piece of folded paper from the waistband of her skirt. "It seems to be a list of deliveries over a six-month period."

"Could I see?"

Cathy obliged while Lady Darriby-Jones looked for her spectacles, put them on and instantly things became clearer.

Not just the words on the paper, but the entire mystery of the murder that wasn't.

Chapter Nineteen

*T*hey couldn't do anything else that night, much to everybody's frustration.

"We do need to be up early," Lady Darriby-Jones said, once Lady Alice and Alfie had been dragged back into the meeting, citing the vital importance of the current discussion.

"Well, my vote is that we get an early night," Alfie suggested. "What time should we be off in the morning, Lady Darriby-Jones?"

"Bakers are renowned for their early starts, so I think we're talking about being ready at 4 o'clock."

"4 o'clock in the morning, mother?"

"Yes, my dear Ali, you see we've really got one chance and we need to make sure we grab hold of it and don't let go until we've solved this case."

The goodnights took only a moment or two, except in one quarter where Lady Alice and Alfie seem to linger endlessly.

"Come on, you two, you won't get to bed before we have to get up at this rate."

"Sorry, mother."

"Sorry, Lady Darriby-Jones."

"If you have an occupation that requires you to be up at four o'clock," Lady Darriby-Jones said at four o'clock in the morning, "then you have my heartfelt sympathy. It's most certainly not a nice time of day."

"In Lord Darriby's brother's day, milady, I was often required to drive people home at four or five in the morning," Smith said.

Lord Darriby's brother had been a wildcat. Sadly deceased at the Battle of Mafeking, somewhere in Africa, Lady Darriby-Jones believed he would have proved a very different man at the helm of the Darriby empire; his death had meant her husband had inherited, but she would prefer to have been several rungs lower on the ladder and have the brother still alive, because she knew how much her Darriby had cared for his brother.

"Shocking," she said, tucking the rug Smith had handed her around her thick skirt, chosen for the occasion, knowing the truth about what Smith said.

"It wasn't always driving home, either, milady."

"I can imagine. Now, all aboard. Next stop, the bakery."

A little later, Lady Darriby-Jones issued the instruction to 'douse the lights, Smith, it's time to buckle down to action stations.' They were parked on a dark street that the bakery loading bay led into, forty yards upstream from the bay.

"How will we know which one to follow?" Alfie whispered, whispering appearing to be the best thing to do, given the circumstances.

"Easy," Lady Darriby-Jones whispered back, "we follow the smallest one. They won't use a big lorry to drop half-a-dozen loaves." It made eminent sense, except without a knowledge of Auchin Bakery's fleet of vans, how would they know which vehicle took the title of the smallest delivery van?

Except, it was obvious. In fact, it wasn't a van at all. It wasn't even a motor car. The motorcycle and sidecar came out last, just as they were starting to give up.

"Go, go, go," squealed Lady Alice, suitably excited. And that's exactly what Smith did.

"Any idea where we are?" Lady Darriby-Jones whispered forty minutes later. She couldn't see in the pitch black but sensed the shaking of heads. "What about you, Smith?"

"Not sure, milady. There's been so many twists and turns and with it being dark, I can't take any reference points. I know we're somewhere east of Auchin. That's about as much as I can be sure of, milady."

"East of Auchin, so, near Cosforth then?" she asked.

"My guess, Lady Darriby-Jones, is we're not quite that far towards the coast," Alfie said, again little more than a whisper, "closer, perhaps, to where we stopped yesterday."

A few minutes later, Smith declared that he was sure they'd just passed the spot where they'd stopped the previous afternoon on their way back from Cosforth Castle. Moreover, the motorbike had moved off the road and he could just about make out its headlamp as it bounced over the heather.

"Ah, I see," said Lady Darriby-Jones, "That makes perfect sense. Stop a little further up the road, Smith, and we'll walk the last bit."

"Walk where?" Lady Alice asked.

"I forgot. You weren't in the land of the living yesterday afternoon after Alfie saved your life by single-handedly catching the dreaded Wolf of Cosforth, but Smith located a cottage or hut on the moor and saw smoke rising from it."

"So?"

"Smoke from the chimney tends to mean human habitation and..."

"You think it's Freddie's parents and they're being held against their will?"

"Precisely. All we have to do is march in there and..."

"Might I suggest another course of action, Lady Darriby-Jones?"

"Of course, Alfie dear."

"That we wait here and only move in when the motorcyclist has departed, minus his loaves and fishes. That way, we can be surer of rescuing the earl and countess quietly and without any difficulty."

"At the expense of letting the culprit get away scot-free? No way," said Lady Alice. To which Alfie pointed out that the 'culprit' doing his own deliveries was highly unlikely. "It will be some junior bod, probably completely unconnected to the person we need to get hold of."

"Alright, you've convinced me, Alfie. Here will be fine, Smith. You might want to turn the car around in case we need to get away and back to Auchin pretty smartish." The excitement bubbled up within her as she issued her instructions.

Heather doesn't make for easy passage in the dark, and it would be night for several hours to come. Several times, one or other of them stumbled as they crossed the half-mile from the layby to the building, which lay amidst two folds of land they later discovered when they returned in daylight; all they had to guide them that early morning was the faint glow of the headlamp and the rattle of a motorbike engine.

But the rattle was getting louder. That only meant... it was coming nearer to them, therefore had changed direction, probably mission accomplished.

That gave Alfie an outrageous idea, and he whispered urgently in Lady Darriby-Jones' ear, or at least the place where he thought it should be, but couldn't be sure in the dark.

"Yes, go ahead," Lady Darriby-Jones replied, wondering why Alfie was talking to the back of her head.

"I'll need Smith's help. Smith?" he called, quite loudly, knowing that nobody would hear them over the motorbike engine. That also meant they had little time. Alfie briefed Smith. Smith confirmed understanding and asked a solitary question.

"How will I know when to move?"

"I'll flash my torch twice," Alfie answered.

It all happened terribly quickly and might have resulted in disaster, except that the heather made a perfect landing platform with its springy composition.

Two flashes of Alfie's torch and Smith rose up from the ground like a banshee rising from the dead, or whatever banshees did in the early morning. The motorbike driver saw this looming figure and darted sideways, skidding on a patch of bare ground and sliding to a stop; the sidecar detached itself and rolled on twenty feet, disappearing from sight into the black night.

But the sidecar wasn't their objective, being empty, they were sure. Within seconds, Alfie and Smith were on the fallen and winded figure, struggling to get up, yet the same heather that had cushioned his fall prevented him from gaining any purchase on the ground, hence rendering him a hopeless captive.

"Let's see what you know about this whole situation," Lady Darriby-Jones said. "Ali, help me get his helmet off."

Lady Alice moved in, anxious to play her part to the extent of brushing her mother aside and taking sole charge of the helmet straps.

"Here we go," she said, lifting the leather helmet without too much care for what lay beneath. "Has anyone got a torch? Let's see who this bounder is."

The collective gasps were louder than the idling motorbike when Lady Alice pulled the helmet off, just as Alfie placed his torchlight on the figure still trying to rise from his grounded position.

"Freddie," said Lady Alice, echoed by all except Smith who, after the initial shock, said:

"Young Master Blythe, what on earth?"

Chapter Twenty

"Slow down," ordered Lady Darriby-Jones, completely unable to take in the babble coming from the Honourable Frederick Blythe, Lord Cosforth, to use his family title.

"I posed as the delivery man, said couldn't remember the directions... where to go and all that. Mother and father... had to find... didn't believe whatever the fellows in the dorm will say."

Gradually, sitting in a circle in the heather, not one of them feeling the intense cold due to an equal intensity of excitement, they managed to extract the story from Freddie.

It seemed that Cathy had kept Freddie up to speed with her discoveries regarding the strange receipts and he had come to the same conclusion that Lady Darriby-Jones had arrived at, namely that twice a week special delivery of several loaves, along with a bag of other provisions, could only mean one thing.

"Mother and father are alive and being held against their will," he said. "It was easy for me to bribe the normal delivery driver to lend me his motorcycle–mind you, it cost me a pretty penny and all my pocket money for this term has gone on the cause. Thank you, aunty, your offer of replenishment is gratefully received. Now, where was I? Yes, you see, with the helmet on, I looked the part and the baker didn't care, just wanted to get his loaves shipped out. So, I was in business, zooming over here, knowing I had to find a large layby on the Cosforth Road, this being part of our land, of course. I knew they were being held somewhere, and I just had to follow directions to get to them."

"Exactly my conclusion, my dear Freddie," Lady Darriby-Jones replied. "We'll make a detective of you yet."

"Well, that's exactly what I want to hear, aunty, for I intend to join the police after school. None of this university lark for me, that's a fact."

Then came the big question.

"Did you find your parents?"

"Rather, but not in too good a shape, I'm afraid. I was rushing away to call for help at the main house."

"It's all closed up," Alfie said, but had to repeat himself several times as Freddie stared blankly at him.

"My home is closed?"

"Yes, clearly some very fishy business going on," Lady Darriby-Jones said, then took charge with a string of instructions in rapid fire, something a sergeant-major would be proud of.

"Freddie, take the motorbike, but you'll need to go all the way to Auchin. Ask at the police station for Inspector MacBride, tell him everything, and ask him to get a squad over to the school quicker than lightning. Tell him I'll meet him there. Can your parents walk over to the car in the layby?"

Freddie replied in the negative, "I think father could, but mother's not so hot, quite a fever."

"Alright, if you can't get the horse to water, take the water to the horse. Tell Inspector MacB to get an ambulance over here."

"Yes aunty, will do."

"What's the matter, Freddie?"

The boy had started to rise from the spot he had tumbled into, but quickly staggered, groaning and gripping his knee.

"Broken bones, super sore, hurts like anything."

She couldn't see his grimaces, but could hear them in his voice.

A proper spanner in the works. The only other person who could drive was Smith, and he was needed to get them back to the school. Would she have to sacrifice being in on the kill in order to alert the emergency services?

Visions of glory vanished from her mind as she contemplated the problem; the safety of Freddie's parents was far more important. She would have to sacrifice Smith to summoning the police and ambulance; that would leave her and the others with a broken-boned Freddie and a set of parents who weren't up to much of an adventure.

Well, they had had more than their share of danger over the last six months; presumably held here in isolation and fed bread and water for the duration.

There was nothing for it. She turned to the others, noticing the first strands of daybreak as she turned to the east to face them.

"There's nothing for it but..." Wait a moment, someone was stealing the motorbike from under their very noses. She struggled to her feet, but too late, the vehicle, minus the sidecar, was pulling away, burrowing a way through the thick heather. "What's going on?" she cried, as the sun poked a few more shafts of light her way, blinding her temporarily.

"It's alright, mother, Ali to the rescue."

"Where? What?"

She turned west, towards the hut in the distance and the others, expecting to see Lady Alice charging around her to launch herself at the motorcycle.

But the voice didn't come from that direction; rather, it blew across the light wind from the east. Nothing made sense.

Then it did. Lady Alice was astride the motorbike, going for the main road as if a swarm of angry bees was after her.

"How do you know how?" she called after her daughter. The wind hindered her question, but Lady Alice had sharp hearing. That same wind helped her reply.

"Barry Baritone has a whole collection," her voice sailed back to the others. "He often used to take me out."

"But have you ever driven one?"

"Not before today," came the reply back, "but now I have."

The voice was lost in the distance between them. A few more moments of bouncing along and the speck that had been Lady Alice astride the motorcycle, turned on to the road. They all watched it accelerate away; evidently, Lady Alice and speed were well-acquainted.

"Alright, what's done is done," Lady Darriby-Jones said eventually, noting that the day had started bright and clear, without a cloud in the sky, but bitterly cold. "Freddie, will your parents be alright to wait an hour or two while we go back to the school and meet with Inspector MacB?"

"Well, they've waited six months, so two hours more won't signify much in their reckoning. I think I can hobble back to your car if I had a little support. What are you doing, Mr Burrows?"

"Checking your leg, Freddie. I don't believe it's broken, just a nasty sprain around the knee. If Smith goes one side and I go the other, we should be able to help you along."

A hobble and a half later, they got Freddie back to the car and Smith held the door open for him and Lady Darriby-Jones.

"Where to, milady?" he asked, just in case events had turned again in the twenty minutes it had taken them to reach the parked car.

"Still the school, Smith, but put your foot all the way down if you will. We're in a desperate hurry.

So, evidently, was Lady Alice, for they passed an ambulance ten minutes before they got to Auchin village.

"That's the one based in the village," Freddie said, "manned by part time volunteers, salt of the earth they are. What do you expect to find at the school, aunty?"

"If we're not too late, I expect to find a fraudster, a kidnapper and a murderer, in order of crimes committed."

"I think we will be in time, Lady Darriby-Jones," said Alfie, twigging on to everything after a period of utter confusion. "I think our target won't want to leave the school, at least not without a fight."

"I hope you're right," Lady Darriby-Jones said as the car swung through the gates and accelerated up the drive. "I do believe you are," she added, as they ran into three police cars parked on the front drive, with shouting going on all around them.

"Ah, Lady Darriby-Jones, just in time for the action." She was greeted by the inspector the moment she got out of the car.

"Major Blythe is holed up in his study with his secretary held hostage. We need someone to talk some sense into him."

That's how, four minutes later, Lady Darriby-Jones, Freddie and Alfie found themselves in the outer office, preparing to talk some sense into the headmaster of Auchin School for Boys.

"I am the headmaster," they heard through the door.

The Mystery of the Murder that Wasn't

"Yes, major, except you retired last year," his secretary replied.

"I was reappointed by all available governors."

"I don't understand, major, with the earl and countess sadly deceased, how could there be a meeting of the governors?"

"Governor, not governors," the major replied.

"You mean?"

"Yes, the last remaining governor, Lord Darriby-Jones. I telephoned him and told him about the sad demise of Mr Hardway. I recommended my services and he said that was just the ticket and thanked me profusely."

"Well, I never," breathed Lady Darriby-Jones, "to think a good half of the mystery could have been solved with a simple chat with Darriby." Then she gathered herself and, together, the three of them walked into the inner study, the scene of Hardway's murder.

There, they found the secretary and the major, but not the latter holding the former at gunpoint. Instead, they were sitting calmly on the sofa Lady Darriby-Jones and Freddie had hidden behind just a few nights ago.

They entered the room and fanned out behind the desk, the major seemingly blind to their arrival.

"You see, I never wanted to retire," he said, as if in the confessional, but now with an audience of five, as the inspector had crept in beside the others, not wanting to miss the show. Lady Darriby-Jones nodded to the inspector and then saw the fifth member, the newly liberated Mr

Robertson. "But my stupid older brother insisted on it, saying thirty years was long enough, it being time to make way for a younger man. After six months of tending my roses, I couldn't take it anymore. I kidnapped the earl and the countess, meaning to force them to reappoint me, particularly as I had heard rumours of grave financial misdeeds under Hardway; theft from the school. Can you believe it?"

"What happened next?" the secretary asked, aware of the presence of others and wanting a full record of these dreadful recent events.

"Well, my idiotic brother was as stubborn as anything, saying I could keep them captive forever, but it wouldn't make a blind bit of difference. I stormed back here to confront Hardway about his stealing the school funds. I admit, I blew my top right off, but I had good reason; the devil of a man had the temerity to laugh at me, laugh in my own face, saying my time is over and he would do what he liked with the school's cash and it was none of my business. I lost it then, went for the jugular and all that. I think I must have expected such an outcome because I was prepared for it, bringing a hunting knife with me. Well, that was the end of Mr Bloody Hardway."

He broke his monologue, looked around the room, and said, "why are you lot here? What on earth do you want?" his questions placed with his best headmaster-like tones.

"Just a little matter of murder and kidnap," the inspector replied, "which my good new friend, Lady Darriby-Jones, has solved. If you would come this way, please sir?"

"Can I just finish the school reports for the fifth formers?" the major asked.

Inspector MacB was about to say no when Lady Darriby-Jones put a hand on his arm.

"I think we may allow the headmaster to finish his work first, don't you think, inspector?"

The End

Afterword

Thank you for reading The Mystery of the Murder that Wasn't. I really hope you enjoyed reading it as much as I had writing it!

If you have a minute, please consider leaving a review on Amazon or the retailer where you got it.

Many thanks in advance for your support!

The Mystery Of Miss Cess Pitt

CHAPTER 1 SNEAK PEEK

Chapter 1 Sneak Peek

Lady Darriby-Jones felt her soul dance for the first time in two months.

Two months in which the whole of Darriby had been battered by storms of sleet, rain and frigid winds. As soon as one finished, it seemed another was rearing its ugly presence, determined to send shards of ice into the hearts of everyone in their community. It had been a bleak winter with nothing much to sing about, no cheer to wind the dreary days in and on. At least, now, in late March, Easter just around the corner, that seemed to be changing.

She told herself she shouldn't be that content with the improving weather, at least not with a difficult conversation ahead of her with old 'Spanners' Workington, the local mechanic and garage owner; he represented a distinct cloud on the horizon, because she had never liked him and had never known how to converse with him; he seemed to see right through the aristocratic skin she had developed over the last twenty years of marriage to Darriby.

She knew him to be a shady character, up to no good in a variety of illegal and barely legal pastimes. Yet, despite Sergeant 'Haddock' Fisher breathing down his collar for years, there hadn't been a single time they could slip the handcuffs on and lead the shuffling, scruffy figure down to the single police cell, known, almost affectionately, as the Darriby Dungeon. Spanners had been clever enough to pay his rent on time every month in cash; Lady Darriby-Jones knew this because the Darriby Estate happened to be his landlord, both for his business and his home, a squat bungalow next door to the garage that seemed little more than an adjutant to the business. There he lived with Mrs Spanners and a collection of grown-up children, all chips off the paternal block.

There were words to be had with Sparky Spanners, the subject being her precious Rolls Royce, banged up in the workshop for well over a week and no closer to being declared fit for duty. Smith, their faithful chauffeur, had tried and failed to make progress towards its reinstatement in the garages at Darriby Hall, so Lady Darriby-Jones had volunteered to take the matter in hand.

Particularly as she had heard reports of a Rolls out and about at night; nobody else owned one in the vicinity, so it became imperative to have a clearing of the air with Spanners and she had put herself forward for the task.

Something she now regretted as she made her way towards his garage.

"It's a fine day," she said out loud, although there was no one within hearing, either to confirm her statement or demonstrate otherwise, "so, I'm not going to let a little cloud over the state of the Rolls ruin this lovely day." This

The Mystery Of Miss Cess Pitt

said with an element of defiance, except she felt strong foreboding as she set out on this task.

The route took her across the lawn and past the sluggery, Lord Darriby-Jones's pride and joy, with its low tunnels and crooked buildings sporting tiny windows and dilapidated rooves; just as well that slugs liked cold, wet weather. As she looked over her husband's empire, she was certain she saw a wisp of blue-grey smoke rising from one corner of the main building as if a witch had taken up residence and was brewing some fearsome spell, making her wonder what fantastic experiments were going on within. Darriby, her dear husband, had been cloistered in the sluggery for several days, barely remembering meal times even.

But that wasn't her concern; she had brought to the marriage twenty years earlier two things, besides several trunk loads of cash and a share portfolio that many would consider murder for. The first was a distinct lack of interest in slugs and Darriby had, bless him, never tried to foist his obsession on her. The second was a great deal of fondness for Lord Darriby-Jones, born of a determination to make the marriage work.

However, fondness had developed into love in about the time it took to boil an egg, not that she had ever boiled an egg, but she liked the expression, nevertheless.

After the sluggery, she crossed a corner of the orchard and then passed the dowager-house, the scene of her first real life murder mystery. Or should that be real dead murder? Poor old Reg Carter had been found battered to death on the grounds; he had come home from the Great War and never spoken again; except he had on his deathbed in Darriby Cottage Hospital, speaking of the 'polite man', hence her calling the whole episode, *The Mystery of the Polite Man*. Lady Darriby-Jones hadn't rested that summer until she brought the murderer to justice. The fact that Frank Useless, ex-policeman and based at Darriby Police Station, had escaped from capture three times and, therefore, never been convicted, was also not her concern; she had solved the crime and then, like any good detective, had moved on to the next one.

To pastures new, except the same old Darriby.

And now they were in the tail end of winter, beating it out like pheasants from the undergrowth. Perhaps the warmer weather would bring another mystery to the steps of Darriby Hall. She sincerely hoped so, feeling the first blast that the sun on one's back produces in springtime, new vigour alongside the new growth around her.

Lady Darriby-Jones picked up her pace as she entered the village of Darriby just past the dowager-house, noting the builders at work to restore the old home where her mother-in-law had ended her days in rather splendid style; of course, not as grand as Darriby Hall.

Rather than lying derelict, she had decided to put the house back in tip-top condition and rent it out. Or, perhaps, Lady Alice could live there if she ever settled down, but that seemed unlikely. She had hopes that her daughter would select Alfie Burrows, the secretary to Lord Darriby-Jones who she had chosen and a top favourite of hers. Yet Lord Baritone had weaselled his way back on to the scene, something to do with motorcycles and the thrill of riding them.

Ever since her daring ride in Scotland, rushing to Auchen Police Station, Lady Alice had been fixated by motorcycles, not to the exclusion of her horses, of course, nothing could ever work them out of her favour. And it so happened that Lord Barry Baritone had a whole collection of them at Baritone House, situated in the bleak but beautiful plain north of Salisbury, where the soldiers played at their exercises.

As she reached the narrow-cobbled streets of Darriby Village, something drove her to extend each stride by four inches so that her legs hit her tighter-than-usual skirt. Millie, her sweet but not so bright lady's maid, had finally persuaded her to leap frog to some new fashions, accepting a narrower skirt, all the rage in '27, apparently. It had been quite a compromise they reached, because Lady Darriby-Jones wouldn't move an inch on the length of the skirts which still reached mid-calf or slightly lower. She now reflected that the combination of length with tightness didn't make it easy when one had to move in a hurry.

"It was considered quite risqué in my youth to show much leg at all," she had told the younger Millie as part of the negotiations.

"Yes, milady, but..."

It hadn't worked; Millie would have to content herself with the narrowing success, accepting that Lady Darriby-Jones desired to stay what she considered, 'acceptably attired'.

Although 'impracticably attired' might be a better description for she definitely felt it harder to make progress as she walked through the streets of Darriby, past the strangely deserted police station and on towards the other side of the village where Workington's Garage lay on the Oxford Road.

Strangely deserted meant all officers must be out and about, suggesting something going on. She pushed forward, aiming for her original destination, there being nothing to direct her anywhere else. In fact, the whole village was peculiarly quiet.

Was it instinct that caused her to hurry and not to question her direction? It must have been on both counts, for, on rounding that tight bend at the edge of the village where the road straightened out for a clear run to Oxford some fifteen miles away, she saw immediately why the police station had been so quiet.

At Workington's, on the left side of the road and fifty yards around the corner, stood a bunch of people, most of them in uniform of one type or another. The presence of the police told her it was a criminal matter, the ambulance, back doors open, told her someone had been injured; the rest could not be deduced from a distance so, naturally, she moved forward towards the scene, her heart fluttering as she stretched her hemline with every step.

Was this... could it possibly be... another mystery?

———

Get your copy of this gripping murder mystery at all good retailers.

Also By CM Rawlins

A Lady Darriby-Jones Mystery Series

The Mystery of the Polite Man (Book 1)

The Mystery of the American Slug (Book 2)

The Mystery of the Back Passage (Book 3)

The Mystery of the Murder that Wasn't (Book 4)

The Mystery of the Miss Cess Pitt (Book 5)

The Mystery of the Missing Ladies

COMING SOON!

Newsletter Signup

Want **FREE** COPIES OF FUTURE **CLEANTALES** BOOKS, FIRST NOTIFICATION OF NEW RELEASES, CONTESTS AND GIVEAWAYS?

GO TO THE LINK BELOW TO SIGN UP TO THE NEWSLETTER!

https://cleantales.com/newsletter/

Printed in Great Britain
by Amazon